D0066172

So Much a Part of You

So Much a Part of You

Stories

Polly Dugan

Little, Brown and Company

New York   Boston   London

The characters and events in this book are fictitious. Any similarity to real persons, living or dead, is coincidental and not intended by the author.

Copyright © 2014 by Polly Dugan

All rights reserved. In accordance with the U.S. Copyright Act of 1976, the scanning, uploading, and electronic sharing of any part of this book without the permission of the publisher constitute unlawful piracy and theft of the author's intellectual property. If you would like to use material from the book (other than for review purposes), prior written permission must be obtained by contacting the publisher at permissions@hbgusa.com. Thank you for your support of the author's rights.

Little, Brown and Company
Hachette Book Group
237 Park Avenue, New York, NY 10017
littlebrown.com

First Edition: June 2014

Little, Brown and Company is a division of Hachette Book Group, Inc. The Little, Brown name and logo are trademarks of Hachette Book Group, Inc.

The author gratefully acknowledges the editors of the following publications, where these stories first appeared, in slightly different form: *Line Zero* ("A Matter of Time") and *Narrative* ("Masquerades," originally published as "One at a Time").

The publisher is not responsible for websites (or their content) that are not owned by the publisher.

The Hachette Speakers Bureau provides a wide range of authors for speaking events. To find out more, go to hachettespeakersbureau.com or call (866) 376-6591.

ISBN 978-0-316-32032-0
LCCN: 2013957225

10 9 8 7 6 5 4 3 2 1

RRD-C

Book designed by Marie Mundaca

Printed in the United States of America

For Judy Sweeny, my mother

Pride is for men; young girls should run
   and hide instead.
Risk the game by taking dares with "yes."
                10,000 Maniacs, "Eat for Two"

Her sins, which are many, have been forgiven, for she loved much.
                        Luke 7:47

We are all ghosts haunting someone somewhere.
           National Flower, "Fast as Hell"

Contents

So Much a Part of You

The Third Rail

IN THE MIDST of the Depression, in a small New Jersey town overshadowed by the exhaust of Camden's industry and that city's legendarily virulent crimes, John Riley is a smart twelve-year-old boy with a dog named Jerry and a paper route, but he is not a happy child.

His father, Jack, is a drunk who has futilely negotiated for better jobs and higher wages than are available until he has alienated every possible employer and has ceded the family's earning power to his wife. Frances Riley takes on two jobs and makes just enough to sustain the family. Although the Rileys are never warm, they are never hungry. Jack is a sports fan who listens to the Yankees with his beer on Sundays while his family attends mass, but John isn't the least interested in joining his father, who sits rapt by the radio. *You can't hit or throw or really even run for shit anyway,* Jack often says to his son, *on those spindle shanks, for Christ's sake.*

Instead, John loves to take apart and reassemble clocks—he did three in a week once. He does it because he wants to see how the clocks work, because he's good at it, and, secretly, because doing it fills him with a private, foreign sensation of pride—which the church warns against. According to Father Flynn, pride is a sin, far worse than something like not knowing how to build a clock, but for John the reverse is true. He wants to disassemble and reconstruct more complex things too: a radio; someday a car engine. But his vanity and the comfort that accompanies it are tenuous. Mostly he feels the omnipresent shame of not being, and not wanting to be, an athlete.

Unlike John, his sister, Claire, who is three years older, is always playing games and is always out of the house. Roller-skating, bike riding, and climbing trees keep her and her long legs away from home all day during the summer, from first to last light and into the autumn's abbreviated days. Even the fleeting winter hours of sun keep her outside more than in.

The afternoon of Claire's fourteenth birthday, John watched their father stand behind her while she sat at the dining room table writing a thank-you note. Jack slipped his right hand down Claire's blouse and cupped her left breast.

"That seems about right," Jack said. He extracted his hand and walked out of the room.

For the next ten minutes—John saw the time pass on the breakfront's clock—Claire stared at the wall across the room from where she sat before she resumed her writing. Ever since that day, she spends less time at home and more of it away.

A father will do such a thing to his daughter, John concluded after what he saw, but not to his son. His father doesn't touch him. Even when John is punished, the belt does all the work. He is anxious anticipating the strap, but once his father starts, he doesn't flinch.

The Rileys have one bathroom, and it seems to John that whenever he needs to use it, sometimes badly, Claire is already locked inside. When John tries the knob, she scolds back, "I'm in here. You can wait."

"I have to go," John says. "Hurry up."

"When I finish," Claire says. "I'm not finished."

If he can, he waits, but if he can't hold it, he'll go outside, knowing if his parents found out, they'd punish him. When he has to sit on the toilet, he'll threaten Claire with getting their mother, and she'll either ignore him or shout from the other side of the door, "You're a pansy," and John will do the best he can.

But one day John, desperate, shouted back, "And you're a useless bitch." His father had called his mother that one night at dinner because of the roast. He'd been to the pub early and had come home in a foul mood.

"This meat is like cowhide," he'd said. "Goddamn, you're a useless bitch."

His mother had continued eating—they all did—as though he hadn't uttered such a thing.

Claire opened the door and stared at John. "What did you say?" she said. She was four inches taller than he by then and looked down at him when she spoke.

"You heard me," John said. "You're a useless bitch."

Claire shoved him hard with both hands, and John, not expecting it, hit the wall on the other side of the narrow hallway.

"You know what?" John said, recovering and standing up straight. "You're stupid, too. Hit me again if you want. You'll still be stupid and you'll still be a useless bitch."

Claire walked away, but before she did, she said, "And you're still a pansy."

Because of Claire's monopolizing of the bathroom, and how she tortures him with it, John has no shortage of anger for his sister, but one night when his parents fought in the living room, his anger softened, and he's tried to remember that feeling when he thinks she is being simply hateful.

It was close to ten o'clock, and John was reading in bed. He heard the front door slam and then the collisions against the floor and living room walls. He got up and looked across the hall into Claire's room. It was empty.

He crept downstairs and stood at the bottom of the stairwell. When he peered around the corner into the kitchen he saw Claire crouched under the table. Her knees were tucked up against her chest, and her arms were wrapped around her legs. The only light in the room came from the small lamp over the sink. John listened to his parents in the living room and watched his sister listen, too.

"Pick yourself up," his mother said. "Stand up."

"You hopeless bitch," his father said. "Get out of my face. Get away from me."

"You're worthless," his mother said. Her voice was cold and even. "Disgusting. I said stand up. Get out. I don't want to see you again until you're not falling down."

"This is my goddamn house," his father said. "You fucking bitch."

"This is my house!" his mother shouted. "Get out." John heard the door open, more noises, the door close, then quiet.

After it was over, John could see Claire's body shaking, but she didn't make a sound. He had heard and seen enough and went back to his room.

The next morning, after he was dressed, he knocked on Claire's door.

"What?" she said.

"It's me," John said. "Can I come in?"

"Go ahead."

When he walked into her room, which he rarely entered—he couldn't remember the last time he'd been inside—he was surprised to find her sitting on her made-up bed, reading.

"What do you want?" She closed the book.

"I saw you last night," John said. "Don't hide like that. You'll be in trouble if they find you."

Claire raised her chin. "They haven't found me yet. I listen all the time. They've never found me. I wish they would."

"Claire."

"Worry about yourself," she said.

John delivers his papers every afternoon, and Jerry accompanies him. Jerry's arrival followed the death of the Rileys' three unfortunate previous dogs, all named Patty—one male and two females—who were hit and killed by cars before they turned two. Finally, Frances announced that their next dog should have a new name, in the hope of turning their canine luck around. And so, Jerry, a six-year-old terrier mix, has so far survived living with the Rileys, with his luckier name and smirky face.

John's best friend, Tim, one of the seven Murphy children, lives across the street and three houses down. John could get to the Murphys' with his eyes closed, his body knows the walk so well. Tim plays catch with his father some afternoons while John watches or reads. Every time, Tim asks, *Want to join?* and John says, *No, thanks,* as if it's the first time Tim's invited him. Tim will say, *Okay, suit yourself,* and plays with his dad. John's reliance on Tim's quiet, enduring acceptance of his routine refusals is the reason Tim is his friend.

When Tim and his dad throw the ball back and forth, Mr. Murphy will say, *Almost, bud!* or *That was close, son,* and *The last one was tricky and got away from you, Timmy* when Tim misses the ball, but most of the time he catches it. When he does, Mr. Murphy says, *That's an out, no doubt!* or *Got it, sport!* and *You've got an arm on you, all right!* when Tim throws the ball back to him.

When John sits on the Murphys' porch and reads, Tim's sister, Kathleen—the only girl in the family—often appears and sits next to him with her own book. Kathleen is thirteen and a grade ahead of John and Tim. The Murphys call Tim and Kathleen their Irish twins. John couldn't figure out what it meant, so he finally asked Tim.

"Kathleen was still a baby when I was born," Tim said. "She wasn't even one yet. There were other babies that were never born; they died inside my mother." Although John didn't want to know about other babies who were never born, and he certainly hadn't asked, Tim was not in the least reluctant to share this sad detail of his family.

For the first several weeks after Kathleen joined John, she was reading books by Agatha Christie. Then she started *Gone with the Wind.* She and John don't usually talk, but one day John had a book about sundials he'd gotten from the library, and Kathleen shut hers and leaned over his.

"What are those?" she said.

"Sundials," said John. "Clocks for people in ancient times."

They looked at the diagrams as John turned the pages.

"How did they tell time at night?" Kathleen said.

"I don't know," he said.

"Tim says you like clocks. How come you like clocks so much?"

Kathleen's curiosity confused John, but her questions made his face hot.

"I'm interested in time, I guess," he said. "Don't you think it's interesting? The idea of it?"

"I never really thought about it," she said. "Tim doesn't read as much as you. None of my brothers does. I don't know any boy who reads as much as you."

"What's your book about?" He wanted to get out from under her attention.

"So many things," Kathleen said. "The Civil War, a great plantation, Scarlett O'Hara's fight for her home. I think after I finish it I'm going to read it again."

"Why would you do that?" said John. "You've already read it."

"Gosh, same as you with your dumb clocks," Kathleen said. She opened her book and slid away from him. "Because I think it's *interesting.*"

"Sorry," John said. "I didn't mean anything; I was just asking."

"You've never read the same book twice?" she said.

"No. When I finish one I start a new one."

"Well, maybe you should," Kathleen said. "You can miss things the first time."

"Yeah," said John. "I guess."

They went back to reading, and John was afraid maybe she would stop sitting with him after what he'd said, but the next time he was at the Murphys' watching Tim and his dad, she joined him again. She still had *Gone with the Wind,* and John wondered, but didn't ask, if it was her first or second time reading it.

Tim has a paper route, too. The boys each have a portion of the town, and their respective routes start at the intersection of a figure eight and fan out, John going in one direction, Tim in the other. Their routes take them through different neighborhoods, and when they're finished the boys reunite at the same place they started. They compete with each other to see who can finish faster. Although John tosses his papers underhand from the bottom stair of people's porches while Tim throws his overhand from the sidewalk, they are usually fifty-fifty, but when it's collection day, John is always done first because Tim talks to people longer than he does. The routes are uneventful, and John is often bored. In the frigid winter and soggy spring, he is resentful. On collection days, he stops to throw a stick for Jerry in the field they cross midroute, knowing he will finish before Tim no matter what.

John's route takes him over the railroad tracks. The tracks don't overly worry him, because he is a careful boy, but ever since a teenager was electrocuted by the third rail walking the tracks two summers ago, he is painfully aware how close the lethal charge is — so close that he could touch it if he wanted to. It reminds him of the observation decks at Niagara Falls that he's seen pictures of. People could so easily launch themselves over the falls. The proximity of possibility plays on his anxiety. *They could if they wanted to.* He calms himself every time he crosses the tracks with the knowledge that he is better protected from the third rail since the boy died: after the tragedy, a wooden platform was installed that covers the electricity so it can do its job while people — especially those who are careless — are safe from harm.

One rainy April day, he has to deliver not only his route but Tim's as well. Tim has gotten very sick overnight, and his mother, Mary, has asked Frances if John can do Tim's papers. He just saw Tim the previous afternoon; Kathleen, too.

"Can you deliver his, too?" his mother asks him. "It's twice as much."

"Sure," he says. "I'm fast, and I'll start earlier."

"I'll believe it when I see it!" his father shouts from across the room. His father's comments often make his palms sweat, but today he is more worried about Tim than he is about Jack.

"Are you feeling well enough?" His mother feels his forehead. "Dear God, Mary is terrified. Influenza is taking over in Europe. People are dying."

"Those goddamn people don't wash!" rants his father.

"Jack," his mother says. "That'll do."

"Yes, *Mother,*" his father snaps back.

"I'm fine," John says. He wants to ask his mother, *Do you think Tim is going to die?* But he can't manage to utter such a thing.

John and Jerry head out to the slick streets with two full bags. They'll do Tim's route first. Once he's delivering his own, John figures, he'll be tired, but can rely on habit and routine. By afternoon the rain has stopped, but the downpour has left oily puddles, and children splash and bike through them. He passes Claire perched in a tree down the street, reading a book and dangling her legs. She doesn't look up, and John doesn't call out to her.

He wishes he could visit Tim, but the Murphys have shut themselves up in their home to contain the illness. He wonders: if Tim does die, will the loss be easier for his family to bear because of all the children they would have left? Or is the tragedy the same no matter if you start out with seven or with two?

Tim's route feels longer than his own, and John wonders if his is easier or if Tim's seems tougher because it's unfamiliar. One woman wants to pay him, although it's not collection day, which is always Thursday. Today is Tuesday.

"Young man, I didn't pay last week. I owe," she says, beseeching him.

"I'm not your regular paperboy. He's sick," John says. "I'm just delivering for him today; I'm not collecting. I'm awful sorry about that. You can pay him when he's back." He hurries to the next house, the woman's voice echoing behind him.

He finishes Tim's route and starts his almost an hour later than he normally would. Jerry never lifts his nose from the ground and pees on every surface he can. The scents of the new blocks have put the dog into an olfactory frenzy, with each bush, lawn, and shrub more compelling than the last, and John nags the dog to stay with him.

"Come on, you raggedy whelp," he scolds. "Goddamn it, but you're an ugly bastard. I'm not waiting for you." John is forbidden to swear, but he and Tim do it to show off and see how it feels. "Christ, you bloody sod, quit licking your balls and hurry up." John would never leave Jerry behind, and his bravado sounds hollow to him even as he keeps up the stream of abuse. Jerry always catches up, and John knows he will.

By the time he is halfway finished with his own route and they've gotten to the field, it's twenty minutes until supper and Jerry has blissfully followed his nose to his heart's content. John has been going as fast as he has ever delivered a route and decides to stop anyway and throw a stick for the dog, whose energy never wanes.

"Get it, Jerry, go get it!" he yells. "Can't ya run any faster, ya sissy?"

The dog streaks after the stick every time, races back with it, and begs for more.

"You are a funny-looking rascal," he says. "You filthy maggot. This is the last one."

The terrier brings it back, and John takes the stick from him. The dog trots to a nearby puddle and submerges his chin.

John samples some of the phrases he wants to use, his passion for the words winding down. "Come on, you old whore. Hurry up, you son of a bitch. You shitty cur."

He waits for the dog to finish drinking. When Jerry has had enough, he lifts his muddy face from the puddle, licks his wiry beard, and yawns.

"Come on, mate," John calls, then whistles. "We're almost through."

Jerry trots toward him, panting, his tongue dangling like a broken limb, and John turns and heads for the tracks. He really has to hurry now to make it home for supper. *Dear God,* he silently prays. *Please don't let Tim die. Please don't let anyone else I know get sick.* He is tempted to pray that people he doesn't like will get sick, but he knows God doesn't work that way. He looks back at Jerry, smelling around familiar territory, and whistles for him again. Jerry picks up his pace and comes toward John.

The tracks are a few feet ahead. He can't stop thinking about Tim. Is he unconscious? Delirious? In pain? Is he vomiting a lot? John hates to vomit. Can Tim breathe? Will they pray for him at church? What is it like when a kid dies? John didn't know the teenager who died. This is different.

John crosses the tracks and steps over the wooden platform.

"You fucking cunt," he sneers down at the lethal rail after he's walked over it. Every time he crosses it unscathed, he feels defiant and relieved. Saying the nastiest words he knows empowers him. He has heard his father scold the Yankees the same way when they lose.

"Come on, Jerry!" He shouts over his shoulder and lengthens his stride. If he is late for supper, his father will mock him and highlight his weaknesses — unless Jack is jovial. If the Yankees have won, maybe his father will admonish him for having too light a paper route all these months until today. *John!* Jack might taunt. *You've been a lazy mick till now. A boy had to get sick before you'd pull your full weight.*

A scream assaults John's ears and he stops dead. He's never heard such a sound. He spins around, startled and confused. It's Jerry. Frozen. Hovering in space. The dog's left hind foot has slipped beneath the platform and is tapping the current underneath.

He sprints back and wails. "No! Jerry!"

The dog's expression belies what is happening. His teeth are exposed, framed by his beard, stuck in a comical giggle, which would be hilarious were it not for the reason why.

John's heart races, and his mouth tastes like metal. He is terrified — he knows how electricity works. He can't grab the dog; they'd both be done for. He is wearing sneakers but has been walking on the wet ground — his shoes aren't soaked, but they aren't dry.

He sobs a cadent moan, his thoughts reeling. The papers. He still has half a route of papers in his canvas bag. He hears his father's voice: *But your aim is goddamn terrible. Your sister's is better; your mother's, even.*

John steps as close as he dares to the dog. He wads the strap of the bag in his fist and winds up, summons his father, swings, and sends the bag into the dog's side.

"Fucker! You go straight to hell!"

The bag smacks Jerry, and both sail away from the platform, the dog uprooted from the current. When the bag lands, the papers fly out and carpet the patchy grass. John vaults the platform and stands over the dog. He sobs so hard he is silent. His throat is raw.

He whispers, "Please don't be dead, please. Please don't be dead. Jerry, please."

He reaches down and scoops up the still little body and rubs it. *Come on, little fella,* he prays.

John endures the painful wait before Jerry opens his eyes, dazed, and registers John's face peering down at him. Finally, Jerry's tongue flicks out to John and his grin follows, almost, but not quite, the same as usual.

He sets the dog gingerly on the ground, not sure if Jerry's legs will support him. Stiffly, Jerry stands and does a tentative body shake, head first, and ends with his tail stump vibrating.

John's tears are of gratitude and apology as he chatters to the dog, keeping him close while he collects all the scattered and damp papers. Jerry walks slowly but surely, and stays by John. After retrieving the last paper, John clutches Jerry under his belly, and marches the two of them over the platform and on to the second half of his route. He carries the lean little dog the whole rest of the way, whistling, not caring if he is late for supper and unconcerned about his father's opinion.

He promises himself he will tell no one but Tim what happened, as soon as Tim is well again and John can see him. He'll tell Tim the story, and they'll celebrate Jerry for being a wonder dog, and Tim can take his route someday to pay him back.

Maybe, he thinks, when Tim recovers, *I* will *play catch with him and Mr. Murphy. My father doesn't even have to know. I do not have bad aim, either, not when it counts.*

Because he's not told to stop, John delivers Tim's papers for the next three afternoons and each time carries Jerry over the tracks. On the second afternoon he puts a note in the Murphys' mailbox: *Dear Tim: I hope you feel better soon. Your friend, John.* The morning of the fourth day, Saturday, Father Flynn knocks on the Rileys' front door.

Jack answers and invites the priest in.

"Wanted to let you know the Murphys lost Timmy last night," Father says. "God rest that child's soul."

Frances covers her mouth with her hand, and Jack sets his jaw.

"Like a drink, Father?" Jack says.

"A spot," says the priest. "You are my first house but not my last. God help us."

John runs to his room and takes apart all the clocks. He wants to ask his friend, *Did it hurt? Is dying harder than living or easier?* He wants to say to Tim, *Okay, quit it, you jerk. That was a good one; you got me. Sending Flynn over to say you're dead and all.* The clocks occupy his mind, his hands. He has trouble. His tears don't help, but the work distracts him for hours.

At midday, his mother knocks on his door and opens it.

"I'm making lunch. You should come down and eat something," she says. "Terrible about Tim. John, you should eat."

"I'm not hungry," he says. "I'm busy." He doesn't look at his mother and keeps at the clocks.

Frances stands and watches him until she pulls the door softly closed behind her.

It gives John great comfort to control and manipulate the tools that measure time, keep it, record its passing, and wait for no man. He can dissect the clocks and put them back together again, but he can't influence time, can't skip through it. If he could, he would make Tim hurdle over his illness and still be alive. Better yet, he would make Tim stay put wherever he was when he got sick and not be exposed in the first place. When he lets his mind wander back to Tim, he is utterly lost. *Now what? What happens now? What am I supposed to do?* He wonders how Kathleen is. He wonders how Claire would feel if he died.

The funeral mass is Tuesday, only a week after Tim fell ill, only a week after the trouble with Jerry. For the whole mass he watches the thin, black, trembling back of Mary Murphy. After John takes Communion, he passes Kathleen. She is kneeling in the first pew and looks up at him. He thinks about smiling or waving, but both seem wrong, so he just looks back until he's past her row. But he cannot meet her gaze, or Mary Murphy's, when he shakes their hands at the back of the church. *I should have prayed harder,* he thinks. *More.*

John sees Kathleen at school, but they never read together again, and although John can never fulfill his promise to Tim, he doesn't break it, either, and never tells anyone else what happened. When Jerry dies in his sleep at age twelve, mere months before John's exodus from the Rileys' house to enlist in the navy, it afflicts John with a fresh sense of abandonment. Now he realizes that he is the only surviving creature who knows the story.

A Matter of Time

THE SUMMER OF 1976 Anna Riley turns ten and begins taking riding lessons from Kelly Oliver. Kelly is sixteen, an accomplished equestrian, and well known locally as the one to beat. In two years she will win the county's beauty pageant and be crowned Miss New Jersey, but ultimately not Miss America.

Anna's romantic notion of riding makes it far better than anything else she has been offered a chance to try. Her friends play the violin, flute, or piano; take ballet; join Girl Scouts and collect badges; but none of these interests Anna. Her sister, Meg, who is fourteen and an easier sell, does a little of everything. Meg is spending this summer as a junior counselor at a sleepover camp in the Poconos.

When the girls hug good-bye, Anna tells her, "I hope you have a really fun summer. I'll miss you."

"I'll miss you, too," Meg says. "I'm sorry you'll be here by yourself. Good luck."

Anna's mother, Penny, is silently relieved that there is finally something Anna isn't too shy to try and might love doing, passionately, without fear and maybe, just maybe, for the long term. Anna's father, John — a proud man — is quietly delighted that horsemanship isn't a team sport that relies on a group's performance for an individual's success.

The Olivers' farm lies at the end of a long dirt road with miles of soybean fields on both sides. When the crops are summer-high, the lane to the farm appears from the main road to thread through acres of fluttering emerald leaves leading nowhere. But after a dusty quarter mile, the lane spills out onto a wide, gravelly lot, and there the farm envelops visitors with its quiet grandeur. *Well, hello,* say the ancient, towering maples.

The modest house has horse-show ribbons displayed in unlikely rooms: the yellow of third place, won then forgotten, decorates curtain rods in the kitchen and the bathroom. Two glass trophy cases, brimming with engraved silver plates, cups, and plaques of all sizes in varying degrees of tarnish, dominate the living room.

Stalls of ponies and horses line both sides of the two working barns — shy brown eyes blink and velvety noses poke out into the aisles in greeting. Tack rooms emanate scents of dust, oiled leather, and the warm sweetness of horse. The comforting odors of manure and alfalfa mingle and infuse the air. Paddocks are patchworks of nibbled grass and hardened earth. There is a tribe of dogs: Australian shepherds and shelties and collies committed to herding and rallying every car, truck, and trailer onto the property. A swarm of barn cats weaves between people's legs as they exit their cars. To Anna, this is heaven.

The first lesson is on a hot Saturday in early June. Instantly, Anna believes that spending time with Kelly is just like knowing a celebrity. Everything about her is radiant and spectacular—her green eyes and smile and the proud way she presents the farm—even though on that first day she wears cutoff jeans, a YMCA T-shirt, and a blue triangle of bandanna tucked behind her ears and knotted against the nape of her neck. She is as kind as she is beautiful, and as friendly talking to Anna as she is to Anna's mother. That Anna knows someone like Kelly feels like a discovery she alone has made. She vows she will never disappoint her.

The night before, her father instructed her to call Kelly Miss Oliver. "She is your teacher, significantly older than you are, and almost an adult." His lecture was one-sided and brief—impractical advice, since Anna has met Kelly and her father has not. Anna listened, not interrupting or arguing, neither of which her father tolerates. When he finished his instruction, she safely said, "Okay."

Because she can't stop her father's words clattering in her head, Anna decides not to call Kelly any name at all and just doesn't address her directly.

I have managed worse trouble, she thinks. *Like every time I forget to turn off a stupid light.*

I'm sorry, she pleads after her father raises his voice at her. *I forgot.*

Your forgetting costs this family money. He doesn't shout, but the taut wire of his voice implies more danger than shouting would. He punctuates his rants with throat clearing at random. Tense and frightened, Anna waits for more; sometimes it comes — *Anna, "sorry" means it won't happen again. How many times do I have to tell you about the lights?* — and sometimes it doesn't. Kelly's name is so small a thing she'll do what her father says, even if he'll never know what she calls Kelly.

Tempe Wick is the chestnut Welsh pony Anna rides. She is one of the many horses the Olivers own.

"You can just call her Tempe," Kelly says as she pats the mare's rump. "We love the story of Tempe Wick. We would do anything to save this pony, too."

"What's the story of Tempe Wick?" Anna asks.

"Tempe Wick hid her horse in her house so soldiers couldn't take him and use him for the Revolutionary War. She saved him by keeping him in her room. That's really about all I know of history." Kelly laughs and shrugs like she's apologizing.

The lesson starts at ten o'clock and lasts until eleven, and Anna can't believe how quickly it's over. So much happens in that hour. She learns the parts of the saddle and bridle and how to tack up. How to groom the pony and the importance of checking her all over before and after she rides. She mounts and dismounts correctly;

properly holds the reins between her ring fingers and pinkies; positions her body forward in the saddle and wraps her legs around the mare's sides, heels down, toes out. And the very best part: Kelly hooks a lunge line to Tempe's snaffle bit that she holds the other end of while Anna uses her voice and presses her calves against Tempe or pulls on the reins to make the pony walk, trot, walk again, and halt. Kelly explains posting, and Anna tries it first while walking and then while trotting. She stands in the stirrups when the pony's outside shoulder is forward; she sits when it's back. Around and around she goes in her own circle, walking, trotting, and posting within the larger fenced ring.

"How does she feel, Anna?" Kelly says. "You look great! Girl, you're a natural rider!"

Pride pulses through Anna, and, for the first time, ambition: her only desire is to ride by herself, without the lunge—alongside Kelly on her beautiful mare, Tara; through the soybean fields or in a horse show; anywhere. She wants to have been doing this for years already. When she woke up this morning she didn't know this feeling. Now her life will never be the same. *This is what freedom is,* she thinks.

"She feels good," Anna says. "Really good."

After three weeks, it has become awkward calling Kelly no name at all, so with dread in the pit of her stomach and her cheeks hot, Anna decides to tell Kelly what her father said. They are tacking up, having developed a routine.

"There's something I have to ask you," Anna says. "My father told me something, and I want to ask you about it."

"Okay," Kelly says.

"Well, okay." Anna feels her nerve crumbling but knows she can't back out now. She takes a deep breath. "He told me I had to call you Miss Oliver, like a teacher in school or something. But it doesn't sound right to me; it doesn't fit. I just wondered what you thought I should call you." Her voice fades a little with each word, but she manages to get it all out.

Kelly reaches down and rests her tan arm across Anna's narrow back and tucks her lightly against her.

"That was nice of your dad, to think I'm like a *teacher* teacher, but you can just call me Kelly." She smiles at Anna and winks. "If that's what you want to call me. What do *you* think?"

Anna nods and looks at her feet. "Okay." Although she feels unburdened of the weeks of watchful work calling Kelly nothing, her face remains hot.

Anna marks her summer by the weekly lessons, but there is much more to riding than only the lessons, and she loves all the other parts, too. Sometimes she stays at the farm for hours after her lesson to help feed or muck stalls or groom horses and ponies. Kelly's mother is the leader of a 4-H club, and Anna starts going to the monthly meetings. Kelly shows Tara some weekends, and in the dewy mornings Anna and her mother go see them compete and win. When a show is on Saturday, her lesson is often on Sunday.

While they watch, Anna tells Penny, "Mom, that's what I want to do, too. I want to be just like her."

The first time she sees the inside of the Olivers' house, Anna marvels at the glossy tapestry of hundreds of horse-show ribbons that cover every inch of all four walls of Kelly's bedroom and the professional photographs of Kelly jumping her mare over fences at indoor and outdoor horse shows. When she's not at the farm, Anna is busy and content enough playing with friends or going to the library, where she checks out Nancy Drew mysteries and every book she can find about horses. She loves *The Bionic Woman* and watches the reruns, but her world revolves around the lessons.

That summer, Anna's father takes the bicentennial very seriously. Their home is evidence that the Rileys are avid antiquers who value historic restoration. John reverently hangs the Betsy Ross flag every morning and brings it in every night — early if it rains. Each night, as dusk approaches, he announces like clockwork, *Time to recover the flag*. He makes several phone calls and finds a specialty shop where he buys a tricorne, a three-cornered hat, which he sports for the town's Fourth of July parade, whose route passes the Rileys' house. When the firefighters, police officers, Junior ROTC cadets, and fife and drum reenactment corps march past him as he sits in a lawn chair on his marble stoop, John stands and formally salutes four times.

Since June, Anna's mother has always dropped her off at her lesson and either come back to pick her up or waited in the car with a book. One morning in early August, Anna sees her father's car parked in the gravel yard after the lesson. Although the riding is over, the pony is hot and Kelly has told her that Tempe has to be walked until she's cool in order to prevent colic, which can kill a horse. Anna can't see who's driving but waves at the car as she leads Tempe past the two barns and beneath the trees on their regular route, which is about ten minutes. Today, as always, Anna periodically runs her palm over the pony's chest, between her front legs, to check the temperature there until she knows Tempe's cool enough to return to her stall and hay and water and that she'll be okay.

When the pony is cool enough, Anna puts her away and walks to the car. She opens the door and sees her father in the driver's seat.

"Hi, Daddy," she says and gets in the car.

Her father clears his throat but is otherwise quiet. He starts the car and drives down the lane between the soybeans, a part bisecting two halves of untamed hair. The dogs start to escort them, then retreat to find shade. The day is too hot for more than that.

Anna sits with her hands folded in her lap while the heat presses against her face and the silence inside the car engulfs her. The backs of her bare arms stick to the car's vinyl, and she feels sweat slick between her shoulder blades. She looks out her window for the whole trip. Her father looks straight ahead, clears his throat, and drives.

The Rileys live in a three-story brick house as old as the

town, which was founded in the mid-1800s. Rural communities buffer it on all sides, and it's a fifteen-minute drive from the Olivers' farm to the Rileys'.

Her father parks the car in the garage, shuts off the engine, and, still facing forward, clears his throat another time.

"You were late, Anna," he says. "I was there to pick you up at eleven o'clock and you weren't ready. Your aunt Claire was always late, too. She never thought about anyone but herself. You have to think about other people. When I arrive to pick you up, you are to be on time. It won't happen again."

Anna's eyes prickle, and her throat swells. Her mother has never minded waiting a few minutes if Anna needed extra time to finish everything she's supposed to do. "But, Daddy—"

"Don't 'But, Daddy' me," he says. "You will be on time. End of discussion. We're home now."

Anna follows her father through the back door and into the kitchen, where her mother is making lunch.

"Hi, sweetie. How was riding?"

"She wasn't ready," her father says. "She was late."

"Oh," her mother says, less a word than a sigh. She runs her hand over the top of Anna's head and smoothes her hair.

Anna struggles to keep herself tight and close, as though she is protecting herself inside her own fist. She doesn't know what to say or what she can say. Her father sits at the kitchen table with his right ankle resting on his left knee. His arms are crossed and his chin is high. "She has to be on time," he says.

With her mother stroking her hair, Anna takes a breath and plunges her voice loud and fast out into the room. "When Tempe is hot Kelly says I need to walk her until she's cool enough because of colic and I was walking her and that made me late. I'm sorry."

"And was she cool enough?" Penny's voice does not sound directed down to Anna, who is pressed against her mother's body, but across the kitchen to the table where her father sits.

"Yes," Anna says, and she relaxes the fist around herself.

"Then do the walk in time to be picked up," her father says. He goes to the refrigerator and gets a Ballantine Ale. He opens the green bottle and pours the yellow liquid into the antique goblet he always drinks from. "Your mother will get you a watch, and you won't be late. Don't be sorry, Anna, just don't do it again."

"Go get washed up for lunch," her mother says. "We're having hoagies. I'll call you when it's ready."

Anna leaves the kitchen. Behind her she hears her father raise his voice and her mother's murmured replies. She can't hear what they're saying, and she doesn't want to. Anna knows her mother won't win; no one ever does. But she's the only one who can talk back to him. She's not a lightweight.

By the next lesson, she has a watch, her first one. It's a

sturdy and practical Timex with a black band. Although the buckle is on the first hole, the fit is loose and sloppy. Anna and her mother have shopped during the week and bought the smallest one they could find. She likes the weight and movement of it on her wrist, but the fact that she has a watch at all makes her feel like she's doing penance. Last year, her fourth-grade teacher, Sister Justina, explained sin and penance, and when Anna recalls her words, the watch feels shameful and dirty.

That Saturday, her mother drives her to the farm and waits and reads and they go out to lunch afterward. And so it is for the next five weeks and into the new school year: her mother drops her off and picks her up when the lesson is over or at a later time they've arranged when Anna helps around the farm. This is how the weeks ultimately pass, but when she is sitting and waiting for her ride or hurrying to finish the chore she's doing or walking the pony, she is never sure whose car will come funneling down the lane through the turbulent, dry dust. On every one of those Saturdays, she sees the dust swirl first, then the form of an automobile emerging from it, like a figure skater born from smoky dry ice. As the car's murky profile sharpens she can always tell at a glance whether it belongs to one of her parents — if it's the convertible that one of the farm's boarders drives or the truck delivering hay — but her parents' cars are similar to each other in height and shape. Anna and the dogs wait. It's not until the vehicle has completely cleared the lane that she can make out if it's her father's sedan or her mother's station wagon, with the luggage rack on the roof.

On the sixth Saturday, her father takes her to the lesson and drops her off.

"I expect you to be ready at eleven o'clock," he says. "Did you wind your watch today?"

"Yes. I did."

"Good," he says. "What time is it now?" Clears his throat. "Ten of ten?"

"Make it five of ten." He taps the air above her wrist.

"Okay." She pulls out the stem and advances the minute hand while her father watches.

"See you at eleven," he says.

Anna gets out of the car and walks to the barn. Although this is what she loves best and her favorite place, she is hampered by dread and the threat of the future an hour away.

"Hi, Anna, my Anna," Kelly sings out from the feed room. "Ready to ride?"

"Hi," Anna calls back. "Sure." She goes to Kelly, who is mixing grain in the old chest freezer. "Hey, Kelly, my father is picking me up today and he has to go somewhere pretty important right after," Anna lies. "So I really need to be on time."

"Well, okay." Kelly smiles. "We'll try to be on time."

Anna collects the saddle and bridle and grooming kit from the tack room and goes into Tempe's stall. She is utterly powerless. She can't tell Kelly what she knows any more than she can change her father. She would rather not even ride today, although this is the thing she wants the very most.

This morning, as she has every week, Anna rides better than she did the previous week. After the first lesson in June, the lunge line came off, and for weeks now Anna has been cantering. Tempe responds to her legs and hands better every time she rides; sometimes she responds just to her mind, Anna thinks.

Kelly shouts across the ring: "Great! Good, Anna, good! Perfect, that's it. Straighten your back a little, heels down, lower your hands some!"

The lesson is almost over. "You've done such a great job today—let's do a few ground poles." Kelly rounds up the poles and paces them out. It's very warm for September, and although Anna is already sweating, she feels a nervous flush. She looks at her watch. It's 10:45. She wonders how much time this will take. She is worried about being late, but she knows that ground poles are a start to jumping, and she wants to do the poles — of course she does — more than she wants to be on time.

Anna walks Tempe, then trots her, over the poles several times before they finish. She rides the pony back to the barn, and Kelly walks beside them. Now it's 10:55.

Kelly says, "We should start working on jumping if you feel ready."

"Yes!" Anna raises a victory hand in the air.

Kelly laughs and pats Anna's leg, then the pony's neck. "Good work, you two."

As they near the barn, Anna sees the dust from the lane rising. The pony is hot and will have to be walked. She won't not do this. "If that's my father, I'm going to be in trouble because I'm late," she says to Kelly. "But I have to walk her."

"If your dad comes before you're finished I'll just go and keep him company and tell him what a beautiful rider you are. She only needs a few minutes," Kelly says as she feels the pony's chest. She smiles over at Anna, like this is such an easy thing to do.

Maybe it is easy, Anna thinks as she unsaddles and walks Tempe, not knowing if her father has arrived yet, if it was his car raising the dust. Maybe Kelly, with all her charms and light and beauty, can soften Anna's tardiness by bestowing her magic on her father. She'll be late, but in that moment she is hopeful. It seems possible that Kelly can suspend or dilute the perception of time enough so that her father won't notice.

It is 11:05 when Tempe is back in her stall, safe. As Anna walks to the car she thinks, *Good, since it's really only 11:00.* It's quiet except for the gravel crunching under her sneakers and the farm's sounds reaching out from its far corners.

She sees her father sitting alone in the car. She opens the passenger door and slides onto the seat.

"What time is it, Anna?" he asks.

She holds her breath. "Did Kelly come over?"

"I'll ask again. What time is it, Anna?"

"Five after eleven. So actually eleven?"

"According to my watch it's now seven minutes after

eleven. Which means," he says, "you are two minutes late. Miss Oliver discussed your riding progress but that does not change the fact that you're late. This is the second time. Didn't I ask you to synchronize your watch? I won't tolerate this defiance. What did I say?"

Anna crumples. "Be on time, don't be late." Tears creep down her face, but she musters her defense. "I did change the time. I'm sorry, Daddy. I told Kelly—I asked her if I should call her Miss Oliver and she said to call her Kelly—I told Kelly I had to be on time, I did. So she came over to talk to you while I walked the pony. The pony was too hot. I'm sorry."

She takes a ragged breath and covers her eyes. "I just love, really love riding so much and I'm trying to be really good at it and get better at it and I was trying hard to be on time. It was only two minutes."

"You're not trying hard enough. You may as well have no watch at all if you're not going to use the one you have." Her father's words land like bites. Anna's tears and contrition share the inside of the car with the silence — except for the sound of her father clearing his throat.

He drives the fifteen minutes. Though Anna clenches her fists in her lap, she calms herself and measures the passing seconds by telling herself again and again — like a mantra that will save her — *But the pony was cool, the pony was cool, the pony was cool* until they arrive home.

So Much a Part of You

ALMOST TWO WEEKS ago, during Edie and Anna's lesson with their trainer, Floss Williams, on a clear and brilliant October day that belied her misfortune, Anna fell. She was doing the course with Smiley, who is rarely, if ever, smiley. On a bad day he is lazy and pouts, but Anna motivates him the way no one else can, and she'd always rather push a horse than hold one back. Smiley's show name is "Look Sharp!" like the Joe Jackson song, and when he is on he is breathtaking, and no one can beat them. The horse stands 16.3 hands tall and is a dark bay with a white snip on his face and socks on both hind feet. Anna loves him, even when he's a brat, more than anything on earth. She's never had a bad fall until now, and it wasn't that bad, not for her, because she doesn't remember it.

"Well, he stopped at the fence, and you didn't," Edie told her.

Smiley refused the 3'6" oxer — a jump with two rails, the first one lower than the second, and a width of eighteen inches between them — and over Anna soared. Floss rushed her to the hospital, and Anna's mother, Penny, met them there. She had a concussion, but there was nothing broken — nothing except some missing bricks of memory.

Tonight, the girls walk through Edie's neighborhood after dinner. It's early, but the sky's light scurries away. Six years ago, in fifth grade, they became best friends when Edie started riding, too, a few months after Anna. Edie's father, Leo Beckett, an orthopedic surgeon, walked out on Edie's mom and their six kids the day after Edie's eleventh birthday, and that year she got a pony. Anna knows Edie hates her dad and her birthday, but she loves riding, and has ridden ever since. Edie calls what happened *making lemonade from having an asshole for a dad.*

Anna has never met Leo Beckett, and although she wants for Edie's family to have been spared what happened, it worked out well for her, so it's hard to wish for something different. Right after he left, Edie told Anna, *He was never around much anyway, and I didn't have a horse then, either.*

Anna remembers things like this, but since her accident she has what the doctor calls "some missing data" from her memory. Edie has assigned herself the job of tutoring Anna in her own life, trying to bring her back to where she was before the fall, and Anna has let her. What else is she going to do? Anna knows that once Edie decides something, that's it.

While they walk, Edie doles out details about Anna's own father, John, who drinks every night except when he gives it up each Lent. On Ash Wednesday, that's it — nothing again until Good Friday. All that is months away, but he's not drinking now, and this is the only way Anna remembers him. He hasn't had a drink since her accident.

"We love Lent," Edie says. "We hate Easter."

Edie is more like a sister than a friend, and she and Smiley are Anna's two favorite things in the world.

The darkness intensifies as the girls walk. Edie has been prattling nonstop, as if Anna is in a coma instead of just a little foggy. The hedges they pass have not been trimmed, and they narrow the sidewalk, so Anna follows Edie until the hedges end. Then she stops and listens to the lecture about her own life.

"And so Easter sucks, you know, because your dad starts drinking again and that's no picnic. Lent is supposed to be all this *suffering*, but it's nothing like that. Lent is so *great* at your house! I mean, really. Do you remember your slumber party when we were in seventh grade? You probably don't, but it was during Lent and your dad was so funny and nice and I couldn't believe it because I'd been to enough dinners at your house to know what he's like normally.

"And now of course they're not letting you ride and I don't know what's going on and your dad's not drinking. What the hell? I bet it's him and not your mom who won't let you, but if you think about it I'm sure they're both scared because a fall like that, well — maybe you could have died."

Just to mess with her friend, Anna crouches into the hedge, hiding in the expanding dark. Half a block away from her, Edie stops talking and turns around.

"Anna? Anna!"

Anna hears Edie's panic as she runs back on frantic feet.

"Anna!"

In this instant she is flooded with guilt. The best part of this walk, which she feels as though she's just ruined, is that Edie knows so much about her and is her friend anyway. Edie wants her to remember and be well again. Edie is trying to take care of her, and Anna has been a complete child in return, hiding so Edie will worry. She knows Edie is already worried.

"Hey, sorry. I'm right here," Anna says. She stands and steps away from the hedge. "I must have gotten lost for a minute."

"Shit. That's not funny," Edie says. "You know you can't just use that whenever you want."

"I am sorry," she says. "I'm just so sick of this. There's nothing wrong with me. Nothing, really. All I want to do is ride. I remember how to do that. And I remember the slumber party, too."

"See?" Edie says and puts her arm around Anna's shoulders. "You're okay."

*　　*　　*

The next day, the girls eat lunch during fifth period. This weekend is homecoming, so it's a short school week, and they have the next two days off. Tonight they are working on their junior class float. They are the class of 1984.

"Monica and that crew will be there, because they live for this shit." Edie hums and wears an unfocused, dreamy expression while she takes a bite, chews, and swallows. "I don't know about the guys, though. A float seems like such a girl thing, but remember last year the Saints talking about how they worked on the float?"

The Saints is their nickname for the two coolest boys in their class, Chris Faherty and Jean Baptiste Kelly, who play soccer in the fall and lacrosse in the spring.

Anna does remember talking to them at last year's game and the gray day teasing snow. The Saints and she and Edie were standing in a tight square to stay warm. Sandwiched between the boys, Anna felt like she was lurching down a steep hill.

"No, I can't remember. Remind me," Anna says. She wants to relive it with Edie. She doesn't often pretend like this.

Edie puts her sandwich down and folds her hands on top of the table. "Well, Chris said to me, 'We went to work on the float one night, and there were no cool girls there. You can't ride horses all the time, can you?'"

"He did not say that," Anna says. She can't remember

that part of the day, which worries her now. Maybe she is worse than she thinks.

"Yes, he did, too; you weren't there. It was after the game, and you were in the bathroom or something, but I told you about it—I thought I did, anyway. God, I have so much work to do with you."

"Oh," Anna says. "Was it ridiculously cold last year? For the game?"

"Yes, yes, it was," Edie says. She taps her palms together. "See? You do remember, probably even more than you realize. And it's coming back. The rest all will, too. I know it."

"Don't give up on me; I'm not hopeless. Not yet, anyway."

"Not a chance. You're stuck with me."

That night Edie picks her up and they drive out to the country, in the opposite direction from Floss's farm, to a barn where the float is under construction. Inside, it's like a factory. Some kids are standing in groups talking while others work on the float. Four boys toss a Hacky Sack. A teacher, Mrs. Hickman, hustles through the groups trying to break up the ones milling about and herd them into productive teams. Their class sponsor is Gordon's, the town's sporting-goods store, and so far the float is a half-naked, half-tissue-papered chicken-wire behemoth in the shape of a sneaker.

Mrs. Hickman walks over to them, consulting a clipboard. "Edie, Anna! So glad you came out tonight!" she says. "We could use some help on the laces and sole if you want to get some paper and start stuffing. It's going to be terrific when it's done. Really neat." She points to a table. "Over there you'll see a guide to what color paper goes where and find a pile of precut squares. Dive in! Let's get the shoe under way!" She gives them light fist taps on their shoulders, as though this is all they need for inspiration.

"Let's work on the sole," Edie says. "It will be easier to see who comes in and to talk to people if we want."

They punch the gray tissue through the chicken wire, square after square. It's merciless work, and after a while their fingers are raw and numb.

"God, I need a break, don't you?" Edie says.

They leave the barn. Low clouds, like down, blanket the sky. It's colder than it was when they arrived, and they can see their breath.

"It's not so bad, right?" Edie says.

"Did we miss it?" A voice calls from the open window of a car.

"Who's that?" Edie calls back.

The girls take their time walking. Chris is at the wheel of his mother's station wagon, sucking on an empty Coke bottle. Jean Baptiste nurses a can of Pabst.

Edie leans her palms against Chris's door and peers into the car. "You know, you have to actually go inside for people to think you helped. We may have even gotten in a yearbook picture, so our work here is basically done."

"Well, take a break, then," Jean Baptiste says. He moves to the backseat and leaves the front door open. Edie gets in the front, and Anna sits behind Chris.

"You want a beer?" Jean Baptiste asks them.

"Sure, okay," says Anna.

"Thanks," says Edie.

For the last two years, Anna has thought that Jean Baptiste is simply and desperately dazzling—with his black hair and lean soccer body—like too bright a light. He talks to her the same way he always has, but lately she has become self-conscious when looking at him directly and can rest her gaze on him only for a few seconds before she has to turn away. She wishes such an exquisite boy did not have such a holy name. It doesn't help.

"How is it in there?" He finishes his beer and opens three more cans and hands the girls theirs.

She is grateful for the dark between them. "It's okay, I guess. Kind of cool, you know, the enormous sneaker, and also kind of lame. Some people are into it."

He takes a pull off his drink. "Yeah, well, it's got to be better than the freshman float. Their sponsor is Angelo's Pizza. My sister said theirs is a slice of pizza, levitating in the clouds, like it's supposed to be such heavenly pie. More like possessed pie, I'd say."

Anna laughs, swallows wrong, and sprays beer from her nose. She opens the door and spits the rest on the ground. She staggers from the car. She laughs so hard there's no sound.

Jean Baptiste hurries out behind her. He giggles and runs his hands through his hair.

"God, sorry, are you okay?"

Polly Dugan

All she can do is nod until there's no laugh left in her. Finally, she leans against the back of the car, gasping. "That was so funny. Poor freshmen."

"What the hell are you guys doing?" Chris yells. "I am a dead man if you spill beer in my mother's car."

"Nothing, man — as you were," Jean Baptiste yells back.

"Hey," he says to Anna. "Are you okay?"

"I'm fine," she says. "I haven't laughed like that in a really long time."

"No," he says. "Like, are you okay after, you know, when you fell? Monsignor had us pray for you at mass."

He is the first one to say anything to her about it. Everyone knows — all the parents and the classmates she has known her whole life — so why does she feel so cloaked in shame? She feels naked and shy that he has asked.

"I'm okay. Riders fall. There's a little bit I can't remember, but Edie quizzes me every day like I don't know who I've gone to school with since first grade. She's like a part of me, so she knows practically everything about my life."

"Yeah, how's that going? What can't you remember?"

"If I knew, I wouldn't have a problem, right?"

"Right," he says. He replies away from her, toward the barn, and regret taunts her.

"Hey, sorry. I feel like a freak, you know? You're the first person to ask me about it." She looks away from him and inspects the cuff of her sleeve.

"Are you kidding me?"

"They don't know what to say, maybe," she says. " 'Cause

44

it's weird, right? I don't care. But my parents won't let me ride. That's worse than anything else."

"I bet. That sucks. You're pretty good, huh?"

"Yeah, I am." She smiles in the dark. "Edie's the only one I ever worry about beating me."

"Maybe I can see you ride sometime," he says.

"If I'm ever allowed to again. Sorry for being a smart-ass."

"No problem," he says and taps her shoe with his foot. "I think I can handle it. You guys going to homecoming?"

"I guess. Everybody goes, right?"

"We have a game that morning, but we'll probably go. Look for us."

"Okay," she says. "I will."

"Hey, man," Chris calls. "We gotta split if she's ever going to let me use this car again."

"He'll have a baby if he doesn't get his mom's car back. I'll see you later, Anna." He pokes her shoulder with his finger.

Edie gets out of the car, and Jean Baptiste takes her place. Chris honks, Jean Baptiste waves, and they drive away, the car's tires crunching over gravel as it lumbers through the darkness. The only thing Anna can think about is that Jean Baptiste touched her twice, even if it was just a tap and a poke.

As soon as they get in her car, Edie is already scheming.

"I think this weekend is going to be great. What did you guys talk about?"

"Nothing, really," Anna says. "He asked about the accident. We were laughing about his sister's float. He's so cool."

45

"Uh, yeah," says Edie.

"He told me to find them this weekend," Anna says.

"I know!" Edie croons. "I think something's going to happen!"

"He's so cute, I can barely look at him, though," Anna says. "I can't imagine him liking me."

"Oh, for God's sake," Edie says. "Shut up."

When she gets home, her parents are waiting up.

"How was the float?" her mother calls from the living room.

Anna sits down on the couch next to her. Across the room, her father is reading in his chair. Only reading; not drinking, too.

"Okay. It was pretty cold out there. I guess it looks good."

Her mother picks up one of her hands and squeezes it. "Were there a lot of kids?"

"Some," she says. "Hey, can I go out to the barn with Edie tomorrow? We have a long weekend."

Her father looks up, shuts his book, and puts it on the table next to him.

"Anna, you're not to ride."

"I know," she says. She answers carefully, just as she would tiptoe past a sleeping infant.

"There's other stuff I can help out with. Smiley is still my responsibility."

Her father peers over his glasses. "As long as we're clear. Are we?"

"Yes," she says. "Thank you. Good night."

"Good night," he says.

"Sleep well; see you in the morning," her mother says.

Anna climbs the stairs and waits at the top.

Her father's voice floats up. "Goddamn horse. That's an unpredictable and dangerous animal. What happens the next time? She breaks her neck?"

"John," her mother says. "She has to start riding again. It's who she is."

"She can sacrifice for her own safety," he says, "for the time being. We all make sacrifices."

"It's not her fault," she says. "I'm sure she feels like she's being punished. She's *supposed* to get back on."

"Penny, can you leave it alone? Can you give it a rest for just one night?"

Anna creeps to her room and undresses in the dark. She pulls back the sheet and blankets and lies on her back. She relives Jean Baptiste laughing. Imagines him leaning her against Chris's mother's car. She brings her left arm up to her face. She pecks at the skin inside her elbow, first with her lips, then tries some flicks of her tongue. She takes a little bite. She practices on the inside of her arm and pretends it's his mouth she's kissing.

In the morning Edie picks her up and they drive to Floss's farm, where Edie's horse, Scarlet, and Smiley board. Floss is a competitive and protective trainer and tough but magical at getting her riders and horses to do things they never thought they could. Both girls have blossomed into fierce competitors because of Floss. With her sheer belief in them, she makes the riders as they make the trainer. Every show the girls compete in, they are the ones to beat, and all the other trainers and riders know it. If Floss's girls are there, third is usually the highest that other competitors can hope to place.

At the barn, Edie tacks up Scarlet and heads out to the ring. Anna tells her she'll be right out. Smiley's at the far end of a back pasture, and when Anna calls him he lifts his head from grazing and stares at her before he trots over. When they look at each other like this, she believes in God.

She plans while she walks Smiley into the barn. The blacksmith, Charlie Vandergrift, will be at the farm next week to shoe the horses, so even if she can't ride she'll come out then, too, to hold Smiley. She shivers; the weather will be getting cold for good soon; she can smell it in the air.

Anna tacks up Smiley, finds a lunge line, and joins Edie. With Edie on Scarlet and Anna on the ground, it's the loneliest she's ever felt. Edie rides and Anna lunges Smiley for the next half hour.

"It's weird, huh?" Edie says.

"Stupidest fucking thing," says Anna.

After Smiley is back in his stall, Anna digs through the trunks in the tack room for his winter blanket. She finds it and lays it out to check for tears. There are places where the webbing for the clips has to be restitched. She bundles the blanket against her and walks to Edie's car. Edie always locks her car, even at the barn, and Anna teases her about being an old woman.

"Yeah — one whose car will never get stolen," Edie snipes back.

Hugging Smiley's blanket, Anna leans against the car and waits. A gradual hum makes her look up at the brilliant, unblemished sky. Two planes — fighter jets, maybe — are flying in tandem. Their hum builds to a buzz as they fly higher. The buzz increases until it cracks into a boom, which Anna feels through her bones. She rocks, and something inside her head stings and rattles.

Then Edie is next to her. "Anna, why are you crying?" The horse blanket is on the ground, and Edie has her hands on Anna's shoulders, propping her up and keeping her feet on the ground. Anna feels like she could take off any minute, drift up and float away.

"Did you hear those planes?" She wipes her face.

"Yeah. They were loud, huh?"

"They scared me," Anna says.

"Well, they're gone now," Edie says, searching the empty sky.

Although the upset Anna feels is familiar, she can't quite place it. She feels sick and stupid. More stupid than sick.

"You're okay," says Edie. "Come on, let's go to McDonald's."

The night of the homecoming dance the girls wait outside the gym with groups of other kids standing around. No one goes in right away.

"Maybe I should have parked somewhere more obvious,"

Edie says, craning her neck and scanning the street up and down and back again.

"Hey, hey." Jean Baptiste bounds up the concrete stairs. "Come on, time for a little tailgating. How was the football game? We would have been back but our soccer game went into overtime."

"We lost again," Edie says. "In keeping with tradition." Despite a winning record, their football team loses the homecoming game every year to the same rival.

"Bummer," he says. "We won ours."

"Our float got honorable mention," says Anna. "That was a thrill."

"No doubt," says Jean Baptiste.

Chris's mother's station wagon is parked under a street-lamp on a quiet block around the corner from the school. Chris is in the driver's seat, drinking a Pabst. The engine is off, but the radio plays Led Zeppelin's "Fool in the Rain."

"Get in, get in," Chris says.

Edie gets in the front seat, and Jean Baptiste slides in the back after Anna.

"Grab a cocktail," Chris says. "Help yourselves; have as many as you want. This is it for me." Jean Baptiste reaches into a cooler in the way back, pulls out three beers, and passes them around.

"Hey, Anna." Chris rotates to face her, like a parent who's just pulled the car over, and speaks to her from the front seat. "Jean Baptiste was talking about you the other day."

"Easy, man," Jean Baptiste warns.

"He was telling me," Chris continues, louder, drowning him out, "about your memory thing, and I was thinking about how I could help."

Anna takes a sip and looks at Jean Baptiste. He rolls his eyes and shakes his head.

"Seriously," Chris says. "That would be the worst thing, right, forgetting your life, who your friends are, all your favorite stuff? So, about me, my dad is a cop, my mom drives me crazy, my sisters are nuts. I live for soccer."

"I know, Chris," Anna says. "Thanks. It's not everything. It's just a few things."

"Well, good," Chris says. "I want you to know I always do my drinking at home or on foot. After all the shit my dad's seen. He would kill me if I drank and drove. Another good reason to have me around. That's all I'm saying."

"I'm glad we're in such good hands," Anna says.

Chris pulls a joint from his pocket, lights it, and takes a hit before passing it to the rest of them. "I'm good."

The other three toke until it's gone.

"Let's go," Chris says. "I don't want to sit here all night. Everyone lock it, please."

"*Thank* you!" says Edie.

The four of them start walking, and Jean Baptiste and Anna linger behind Edie and Chris.

"You okay?" he says.

"Oh, yeah," she says. "Quite okay."

"Just checking."

"Looking out for me?"

"Yeah. I'm a saint."

She laughs.

"What?" he says.

"You are, right, *Jean Baptiste?* I want to call you something else. Really badly."

As they walk the space between them shrinks until their hands graze. Without missing a beat, he laces his fingers between hers.

"You can call me whatever you want," he says. "Make up your very own name just for me."

Inside the gym, the first notes of "Comfortably Numb" draw kids off the bleachers, and they ply into couples. Jean Baptiste leads her out to the middle of the dark dance floor to join other pairs, swaying under flashing lights. Anna lays her forearms on his shoulders and rests her thumbs against the smooth, knobby vertebrae at the base of his neck.

He smells like booze, something harder beneath the beer. She knows it well. And more — laundry detergent, shampoo, and himself. His sunny, earthy smell of boy makes her feel empty and reckless. His scent is like a plateful of something she wants to cut up and shovel in by the forkful until she's stuffed.

He links his hands around her waist. "I think about you sometimes," he says and pulls her against him. "It's nice."

This is the first time a boy has pressed himself against her, but she understands the stiffening inside his pants. A ripple, which starts in her stomach, surges down between her legs.

"I think about you, too," she says.

He exhales. He shifts his hands and slides each index finger inside both back pockets of her jeans. Their feet shuffle in a circle as their bodies lean into each other. For the whole dreamy song, every part of her that touches him feels ignited. All they do is dance, but still, Anna is grateful that she has practiced kissing on her arm.

The next week the girls go to the barn and hold their horses for Charlie while he shoes them. Charlie is Dutch Cooper's apprentice farrier, but always does the horses at Floss's. He's young and funny and gossips with the girls while he works.

Anna gets Smiley while Edie goes for a quick ride.

"What's new in your life, Anna?" Charlie asks. He bends over and pulls nails from Smiley's back hoof and slides off the shoe. The horse stands and dozes. Charlie makes everyone relax.

"Oh, well, I had a bad fall a few weeks ago. My parents aren't letting me ride. It's cool to be out here anyway, though," says Anna.

He stands up by Smiley's rump. "Wow, Anna, I'm sorry to hear that, kiddo. Are you okay?"

"Yes mostly from the fall; no from the not riding." Her eyes fill, and she turns away from him. "You know when something is such a big part of you? Without it, you can wonder who you are a little."

Charlie has bent over again and is working on the other

side. "I know what you mean. That's got to be tough. Has Floss talked to them? Do they want you to give it up? Sorry, kid. I hope things change soon."

Anna is glad she said something, and her eyes stop tearing. What a rich life she has — people like Charlie and Floss and even her friendship with Edie. Her life wouldn't be the same without riding.

"I betcha they'll get better," Charlie says. Then a crack surges through the air, jolts her body, and screams in her head.

When she jumps, Smiley startles and throws his nose back.

"Whoa!" Charlie calls from the back of his truck. He is at the anvil, hammering Smiley's shoe. "You okay? Just banging on the first one."

Anna knows now it's the sound of metal on metal that stung into her head, but her heart is racing and her palms are wet. She wasn't expecting the sound or her reaction.

"Sorry," she says. "I'm okay; it just surprised me."

"You got 'im?" Charlie says.

"Yeah," she says, composed and ready for the remaining noise. "I'm good. Sorry about that." Again, the familiar upset she can't place consumes her.

" 'S all right," Charlie says.

On the drive home, she almost tells Edie what happened with Charlie. But they don't tell each other everything all the time — mostly they do, but not always. Instead, she thinks of something else.

"Hey, what if I rode anyway?" Anna says. "If I keep coming out with you they'll never know."

"Yeah? And when they find out they'll kill us both," Edie says. "You don't think they'll find out? You don't think your dad will know the second you do it?"

"I think by the time they do it won't matter."

"Nice knowing you," Edie says.

"Shut up," says Anna.

Anna is home alone studying for a history exam the following afternoon. When the doorbell rings she squints through the peephole at a man she doesn't recognize. She leaves the chain on and opens the door.

"Yes?" she says.

"Here to fix the window."

"The window?"

The man, while not rude, speaks to her like she is slow. "I have an order here from a Penny Riley to replace an upstairs bedroom window." He brings a clipboard close to the door for her to see.

"I'm sorry," she says. "Can you hang on one second?"

She closes the door, sprints up the stairs, and checks every room but hers. There's nothing wrong with the windows in the guest room and her sister's room. Meg is in her junior year of college, and her room has been undisturbed for months. The books she read over the summer are still stacked on her nightstand. A bookmark sticks out of the one on top of the pile. In Anna's parents' room, a vast swath of cardboard covers one of the two windows.

She stands there feeling as blank as the brown expanse. She picks up the phone and calls Edie. "Hey, can you come over real quick? I'll be on the porch waiting."

"Are you okay?"

"Just come."

"Be right there."

Anna lets the guy in and tells him to come and go through the front door as he needs to; she is waiting for a friend.

She sits on the bottom step and can hear him working. She wants to know what's under the cardboard.

Edie pulls up in front of the house and gets out of her car. "What's up?"

Anna stands. "Come here."

Edie shakes her head and throws up her hands. "What the hell is going on?"

"Will you just come?"

Edie follows her upstairs to Anna's parents' bedroom. They both stand in the doorway.

The window guy turns around. "Girls." And goes back to work.

The casing and frame are propped on the floor, leaning against the wall. The wood is splintered. The bottom pane is a scatter of cracks around a hole in the center. The upper pane is a shattered pattern of missing and remaining shards. The glass clings like incisors in a menacing grin.

"Huh," Edie says.

Anna goes downstairs and back to the porch. Edie follows her again and sits next to her. They are quiet. Anna can feel Edie waiting. Maybe they can just sit like this forever.

"What happened to the window?" Anna says.

"Am I supposed to guess?" Edie says. "I give up. What happened to the window?"

"That's what I'm asking," Anna says. "I'm not fucking with you. I don't know."

They are quiet again, and now Anna waits. "Your dad, maybe?" Edie says.

"Right," says Anna. "So when?"

Edie exhales and taps her foot. She says everything as though it's a question. "Oh, boy. Anna, I don't really know, but I think maybe the night before you fell. But I don't really know what happened, I swear to God. All I know is that you called me. It was pretty late. I was already in bed.

"It was almost ten and you called me and you were crying. It's when it was still kind of warm out. You said it was stuck — your dad was pounding on the window because it was stuck, and he'd hurt himself. You said you were going to bed, but you just wanted to talk to me for a minute."

"Then what?" Anna says. She is so tired. Like she could close her eyes and lean back against the step behind her and fall asleep right here.

"Then at school the next day you said your dad got a graft or something. Your parents went to the hospital and you were up almost all night waiting for them. But then it was like a normal day. And then after school we went to the barn, and you fell."

Anna feels like she'll float away. She breathes in and out. Now she remembers. Like recalling a dream — not as soon as you wake up but days later, when something invites it back to you.

Her father wrestling with the window. At an impasse with the swollen, sticky wood. *Goddamn it, Jesus Christ,* he says through gritted teeth. *Motherfucker.* Her mother pleading, losing with each plea. *John, please! Try the other! It's not that warm. We can use a fan!* The slash through the glass, *ping,* the rending of the wood, *crack.* Her father's arm following his hand through the aperture his fist made. The rain of glass on the sidewalk below, *tinkle, tinkle.* Sounds of destruction defying containment. *Goddamn it, Penny! A towel!* Her father's blood on her parents' bedroom floor. Pooling on the hardwood. *We need to go to the hospital, John! Sit down!* Her mother in charge now, managing the mess. Anna backing from the room to call Edie. Sitting in her room, summoning calm. Calm not coming. Her mother leaving her in a rush. The shaky whisper of her voice. *It's late. Can you go to bed, Anna? You have school tomorrow. If it's going to be awhile I'll leave and come back. I'll lock up. I'm sorry.* Her mother kissing the top of her head. Her inability to sleep. Feeling her way down the stairs and getting the broom and dustpan out of the kitchen closet. Sweeping up the glass in the dark. Dumping it into the metal garbage can. *Bang, clatter clatter.* Her parents' return, closer to dawn than night. Maybe she napped. Her mother's voice floating up from the foyer. *You were lucky—very lucky. They said another inch. Less than.* Anna covering her ear with the blanket. Trying but not sleeping. Her mother checking on her. Faking sleep. The bulk of her father's bandage, dominant as a marble pillar on the kitchen table in the morning. Feeling skinned, like a grape, at school. Going through the motions. Glad to be out of the house. Happy to be at the barn with Edie. So tired. On Smiley and in control. Her turn. The horse cantering. What a good boy. Over the wall he takes her. Over the in and out—one, two strides. The turn. The approach to the oxer. Darkness.

How long have they been sitting on the steps?

"Anna?"

Anna grunts out half a laugh. "He put his own hand through the fucking window. He was so enraged. At a window. He was drunk, and no one could talk to him. Then I was just so tired."

"You know I didn't mean to keep it from you, right?" Edie says. "It didn't seem like something to talk about, but I wasn't trying to pretend it didn't happen. And I really didn't know what happened. I didn't. If I had, maybe I would have known what to say. I didn't know if you remembered. I kept waiting for you to say something." Her lips quiver, and she crosses her arms in front of her chest. "I should have come over that night when you called."

Anna looks at her. Now she's taking care of Edie.

"It's okay, you're okay," she says. "I'm okay, don't worry."

Tears roll down Edie's cheeks, and she brings her hands up to cover her face. "I didn't know what to do."

"Yes, you did," Anna says. "You're doing it. Why is everyone acting like something is wrong with *me?*"

They sit there until the guy comes through the front door.

"Window's done," he says. "Can you sign?"

"Sure," Anna says. The guy hands her a copy.

"Have a good day," he says.

Anna leaves a note for her parents on the kitchen table with the receipt. *At Edie's studying. Window's fixed. Be home after dinner.*

When she comes home that night she tells them she's ready: she's going to ace the history test, and she wants to help at the barn this weekend.

"Anna." It's all her father says. He is still not drinking, and this matters more to her than anything he can say.

"I know." It's all she says back.

Edie drives them to the barn on Saturday afternoon. They tack up and walk the mare and gelding to the outside course.

"Are you sure about this?" Edie asks.

"Absolutely," says Anna.

"I'm not," says Edie. "*I* remember what happened. I saw the whole thing. You scared the shit out of me."

"Would you be able to give it up?"

"No," Edie says. "Of course not."

"Well, neither can I," says Anna. "And they can't make me."

"You don't have to jump," Edie says. "Just start slow."

"I was a zombie that day," says Anna. "One day."

"Your parents are going to be furious with me," says Edie. "We're both going to be in trouble."

"No," Anna says. "You won't be. You're off the hook."

"Imagine yourself in my shoes," says Edie.

"Okay, and you in mine," Anna says. "You'd get back on. Wouldn't you?"

"Yes," says Edie, losing. "Of course I would."

"And I'd be worried, I guess," says Anna, "but I'd let you. I'd want you to."

"Well, I'm worried," Edie says. "That's all. I can't let anything happen to you."

"I know," Anna says. "And nothing will. You're stuck with me. Okay?"

Edie nods.

They mount and ride for the next forty-five minutes. They trot and canter, do figure eights, flying lead changes, and work without stirrups. Smiley feels so good to Anna, as though he is grateful she is back. No sulking today. The truth is she was nervous at first, but she couldn't burden Edie, and she knows her horse. He's having a good day. They adjust the rails on the jumps, pace out combinations, and come up with a course. Anna goes first. The sun warms her bare arms between her black leather gloves and her pink polo shirt. Sweat trickles between her breasts, but the horse feels solid between her legs and her hands, and she is not afraid. She and Smiley *go, go, go.* They shine over every jump like a single flawless being. A course like today's is the perfection that wins first place, beating even Edie and Scarlet. After they've cleared the last fence, Edie claps and hoots, and Anna pats Smiley hard on his rump and hugs his neck. Edie has a brilliant round, too, and Anna cheers. They cool the horses, talk about the party they're going to tonight, and muck the horses' stalls. Hang their bridles on their hooks and rest the saddles on their racks.

They drive to Edie's, getting take-out pizza on the way, and shower and dress for the party. A classmate's parents are away, and most of the juniors are there. The house pulses with music and laughter and lights. The stereo is constant. Shots are filled, joints are lit and passed around. Girls dance with each other, and couples make out in dark corners. Boys play pool in the basement. When the Saints show up, Jean Baptiste sweeps Anna away from Edie.

"Get a beer with me."

She feels lucky and special. A pretty girl — a great rider — with an amazing horse. Someone Jean Baptiste singles out. To think about and dance with and get hard for.

At the keg, he fills two plastic cups.

"Guess what?" she says.

"I don't know. What?" He lifts his eyebrows.

"I rode today. It was great; it was really great."

"Your parents let you?"

"Oh, no. Nope. No way. I decided to and did anyway. They have no idea."

"Wild woman," he says, then whistles.

"That's right," she says.

"Cool. Come on," he says. He takes her hand, and they thread through the crowd into the backyard. He leads her to a picnic table and leans her against it. She eases herself up and sits on the top.

"Wow. Anna, my Anna," he trills and brings his face close. His whisper thrills her, and she closes her eyes. When Jean Baptiste's mouth comes down on hers, she tastes his beer and something harder underneath. She thinks of fruit. His mouth is like the ripest, smoothest fruit, a peeled peach or pear. Something exotic. A melon or avocado. As his lips and tongue and hips press against hers, she feels like he is repairing her. Like he is stitching and mending her back together, healing a wound she's been waiting to close so it will finally stop aching. In these electric minutes, Anna decides if he wants more from her than this, she's not going to stop him. The adrenaline, the weight of Jean Baptiste's long body pressed against hers, and the tang of his mouth make her ready to say yes to anything, but all they do is kiss.

She steps out of Edie's car in front of her house at midnight, woozy from lust, pot, and beer. She unlocks the front door and locks it behind her.

"Anna!" her father croons from the living room.

From the foyer, she hears ice rattle against glass.

She is cold and spent and leaves her coat on. She walks

to the living room and sits on the couch across the room from her father.

He is having a drink and reading. His face sports a soft bourbon flush. She knows it well.

"Hi, Daddy." She is more sad than she is surprised. This is what he can't give up, despite the damage.

"Hello, Anna!" he chortles.

"Where's Mom?"

"Told her to head to bed and I would wait up for you!"

"Oh," she says. "Okay. Well, good night."

"Good night!" He sips and returns to his book.

She walks from the room and heads toward the stairs.

"Anna, my Anna!" he sings, and his words float up the stairs behind her. "I'll see you in the morning!" With resolve, she thrusts her hands deep into her coat's pockets and climbs the steps. Both their voids have been replenished. Just as she has been, her father is restored to who he really is. And she knows it well.

Blackball

ON A FRIDAY night in December Audrey Lanigan goes to the fraternity party with the same hope she's had every weekend since the school year started: maybe she will meet a boy and something will come of it. For hours, she and her freshman floor mates drink cheap, watery beer, cram themselves into the line to get refills, dance on the sticky linoleum, and lean against fake paneling having conversations in the dark that last all of five minutes whenever there are breaks between songs or they stand far enough away from the speakers. A new song starts, and Audrey focuses on the nearest wall to lean against, again. As she puts one foot in front of the other, she feels a hand around her waist, pulling her back to the place she is trying to leave.

"Dance with me. Come on, you," the boy says. Her body complies with his steady pressure, and her feet follow. "This is a great song," he says. "I need someone to dance with. I need you."

She knows who he is—a lacrosse player, a preppy and popular senior—and she lets him lead her.

On the dance floor, with his left hand still on her waist, he laces the fingers of his right hand between hers and pulls her close to him.

"You look like you're having a good time." His mouth brushes her earlobe. "I was watching you, and I wanted to talk to you. Good timing."

"I know you. You're Paxton McNally," she says. "I'm Audrey." She lays her head on his shoulder in an effort to stop swaying. He smells so good—like Polo cologne—and she is grateful for something holding her up besides a wall. None of her friends are out here slow-dancing with a senior or any other boy.

Paxton presses his left hand against the small of her back and pushes her against him. "Or Pax, like peace," he says. The two words puff against her hair.

"Peace," she says into his neck. "That's nice. I like that."

"Yeah, you can call me Pax," he says. He hums to parts of the song, and his hand on her back guides her body to mimic the movement of his hips and feet. They move together as one person until Lionel Richie's "All Night Long" ends.

"Let's get a shot and get out of here," says Paxton. "What do you say?"

The dancing and moving against him have recharged

Audrey enough. "Let's," she says. "That sounds like a great idea."

They walk to the bar, and Audrey waits while Paxton weaves between the guys working the tap and comes back with two shots of tequila. No lime or salt. He watches her down hers, then swallows his.

"Where's your coat?" he says. "I'll get your coat."

They leave the party close to midnight.

Paxton is a liability for women, but he doesn't lose sleep over it. He isn't a physical threat. No funny cocktails, no force. He knows no means no. But he is ready to bed any woman who is willing, and he is unreliable and unrepentant if there is any aftermath. His girlfriend, Kira—a Tri Delt, a junior—is in London for the semester, and while she's away, as far as Pax is concerned, any girl who wants to sleep with him goes in with her eyes wide open. He doesn't pretend to be anything other than an attentive, good lay and certainly not anyone's knight in shining armor. Not even Kira's, and her mind-set is not unlike his, which is a major reason they succeed as a couple.

"Your girlfriend's abandoning you this fall, poor thing," Kira had said to him in his bed one morning the previous spring. "She'll go to the Lake District and make a poet fall in love with her." Her elbow dented the pillow, and she cradled her chin in her right palm. Her left hand worked its way up his thigh to his hip, then down. She brought her face close and spoke against his lips. "Right now I can still feel you dripping out of me," she said. "But I might not even like you tomorrow."

"I have a place off campus," Paxton says. "It's a bit of a walk." He drapes his arm over Audrey's shoulder. "Are you up for it?"

"Sure," she says. "It will do me some good. Won't it do you some good? We'll warm up along the way." She leans into the crook of his elbow and looks up at the sky. She blows vapor rings. "God, there are *so* many stars out," Audrey says. "It smells like snow. I hope it snows."

"So, Abby, how come I haven't met you till almost Christmas?" he says.

"*Pax*, you're hilarious," she says. "You're really funny. My *name* is Audrey."

"Audrey!" he says. He releases her and throws his hands in the air, then lays the weight of his arm on her shoulder again. "I knew that. I know your name. It was loud in there."

Audrey laughs. Whether what he said was true or not, it was funny, in a sad way, but she decides it's a small thing. It was a loud party, and maybe he's a little drunk.

"This is a huge school," she says. "You can't know *everyone*." She is sharpening up in the cold. "Especially not every freshman."

"Well, you stand out," Paxton says. "You're hard to miss."

"Oh," Audrey says. "Really?" She isn't sure what he means.

He cinches his elbow tighter around her neck. "Really,"

he says. "You're eye-catching. You caught my eye. You going to rush next semester?"

"Of course," she says. "I love the Tri Delts. The Kappas seem cool, too. I really do love the Tri Delts, though," Audrey says. "That's the only bid I really want."

When they get to Paxton's apartment, he leaves the lights off and takes her coat and lays it on the couch.

"Could I have some water?" she asks.

"Sure," he says. "I'm going to have a beer—you want one?"

"Okay," Audrey says. "And a glass of water."

He brings the drinks to the dark living room and sets them on the table.

"Come here," he says. "God, you are so fucking cute."

He sits on the couch and pulls her by the waist, making her straddle his lap, and kisses her. She kisses him back and peels off his sweater, then his turtleneck, like she is undressing a child. The streetlight beaming through the blinds projects a pattern of slats against his long, smooth body.

"This isn't so comfortable," Paxton says. "Let's move."

He slides to the edge of the couch, keeping her in her same straddling position, and stands, cradling her ass and thighs, and walks them into his bedroom. There is an aquarium against one wall and a lava lamp next to his bed, which is unmade and has dark green sheets.

"Now you," he says. He sits back on the bed with her still on top of him and unbuttons her cardigan and eases her turtleneck over her head. He puts his mouth on her neck and slides her bra straps off her shoulders and unclasps the back. He drops the bra on the floor and reaches down to the button on her jeans.

"Hey, sorry," says Audrey. She grabs and stops his hands. "Wait. Sorry, but I'm just finishing my period."

"That's okay," he says. "A little blood's no big deal." He continues with her jeans and rests his front teeth against her shoulder. "What's a little mess? I like it, if that's okay."

Audrey leans on him and lets him work on her. He rolls her on her back.

"I have to go to the bathroom for a minute," she says. She leaves to deal with her tampon. It's not bad. She doesn't have anything to worry about, but she's still glad his sheets are dark.

After she gets back in bed, Paxton reaches into his nightstand drawer and pulls out a packet he opens with his teeth. "So listen," he says. "I don't want to kill the mood, but I don't want you to get any ideas. I have a girlfriend. Kira. She's in London this semester."

Audrey sits up and covers her breasts with her hands. She leans against the headboard and presses her knees together.

"I don't have any ideas," she says. "I don't want to be your girlfriend. Look what you're doing. What are you doing? I should go."

She slides to the edge of the bed, and her feet find the floor. He wraps his hand around her wrist.

"Wait, wait, hang on," he says. "Don't be like that. I'm not married. She's doing the same thing while she's away, I'm sure. We're having fun, right? I like you. Please don't go; please stay."

"Really?" says Audrey. "I'm not the one with a girlfriend. I don't have a boyfriend. I don't have anything to lose."

"Really," says Paxton. "It's cool, everything's cool. Please stay. Sorry I blew it. Forget I said anything."

Audrey looks at him.

"Just forget it, please," he begs. He sits up and kneels on the floor in front of her. He kisses her bottom lip and traces her nipple with his finger, then gives it the lightest pinch. He pulls her hand down between his legs. "God, look what you've done to me. Can you help me out with this?" He holds the packet between two fingers and hands it to her. "Let's get this thing on," he says. "You are so fucking cute," he breathes into her neck.

He's the first boy she's gone to bed with since she started college, and while she doesn't feel everything he does as well as she would if she hadn't been drinking, all the things he does still feel good. He licks her stomach, and his fingers flick between her legs. All the time he takes before he slips into her and then — still in no hurry — intently starts pushing, steadily swelling and filling her. He works hard to get her to come, but she can't quite get there, so he finally finishes, arching his back and pulling her body up against his when he does.

They are awake until it's almost light, and Audrey isn't

sorry. Not for staying and not for the coffee and breakfast he makes her. He likes her, even if he does have a girlfriend. He likes her enough that she spent the night, and she's proud that he wanted her to.

In the morning, after they've eaten, he clears the plates and stacks them in the sink. He stands behind her and presses his hands on her shoulders. "Hey, I'm going to shower," he says. "How about a shower?"

"That's okay," she says.

"Come *on*, Audrey," says Paxton. "*Please* take a shower with me. I need some company. I'll do your back." He takes her hands in his and walks backward, leading her from the kitchen to the bathroom. Since August, it's the first time she's showered anywhere besides the communal bathroom in the dorm, and after a replay of the night before, he does, as he said he would, do her back.

One night the following week, dead week, Paxton studies in his regular carrel on the third floor of the library. It's in a secluded row, tucked back by the archives and special collections, but he always works in the same place so people who know where to find him can.

Anne Cavanaugh and Caitlin Buckley walk up and lean on the edge of his carrel. They are seniors, too. Caitlin is a Tri Delt, and Anne is a Kappa. They are friends with Kira. Paxton had made out with both of them their freshman year, but nothing more. They had been officers in their sororities.

"Pax, look at you hitting the books," says Anne. "What a good boy you are."

"Buck; Annie," he says and rocks on the chair's back legs. "You ladies passed everything already?"

"Stretching our legs," says Caitlin. "Making the rounds. You going out later?"

Audrey walks around the opposite corner and stops on the other side of his carrel.

"Hi, Pax," she says.

"Hello," he says.

He balances on his chair between Audrey standing on his right and Caitlin and Anne on his left.

"I'm taking a break," Audrey says. "What about you— you studying?" She leans forward with her chin and peers at the books in front of him.

"Right now I'm talking to my friends," he says. Audrey looks at Caitlin and Anne.

Paxton watches her and waits.

"Hi," says Audrey to the two women.

"Hello," they say in unison. They back away from the carrel wall. Anne straightens and stretches. Caitlin yawns.

Paxton clasps his hands behind his head and looks at Audrey. "I need to get back to work," he says.

"Right," says Audrey. She crosses her arms. "Okay, sure. See you later." Her glance encompasses the three of them before she leaves.

Paxton eases the chair's front legs back to the floor.

"Who was that?" whispers Anne.

"No one," Paxton says. "A dumb freshman."

"Another one?" Caitlin whispers.

"She's no one worth mentioning," he says. "I'm not kidding."

"You poor bastard," says Anne. "Kira will be back next month."

Caitlin scolds him. "You're going to have to clean up your act."

"Will you give me a fucking break, Buck?" he says.

"She *likes* you," teases Caitlin.

The last thing he needs is Audrey trying to insert herself into his real life, and he most certainly doesn't welcome the prospect of her becoming a pledge in his girlfriend's sorority. Things need to be managed.

"Jesus, Caitlin, I said give me a break already. I'll tell you what, though," Paxton says. "Next semester, when you're giving out bids, she's not what you're looking for. Neither of you. I'm not kidding. Trust me—you don't want easy little girls like her."

"You're bad," says Anne. She pats him on the head and dishevels his hair.

"Yeah, I'm the worst." He laughs and rocks on the chair's two back legs again. "Why the hell are the two of you even talking to me?"

"Be good, Pax," Caitlin says. She closes his open book, losing his place. "Get back to work."

"I'm serious," Paxton says. "You don't want her. You know I'd tell you if you did."

*   *   *

During rush week in March, Audrey makes it through the first three rounds of parties at Tri Delt, Kappa, and Pi Phi. Six of her floor mates want bids from Tri Delt, too, and, like Audrey, they grow more cautiously confident and excited with each party. They know they are pretty, like the Tri Delts — some of the prettiest girls in the freshman class — and they gravitate toward their own kind, hoping to be recognized.

The afternoon of the preference parties, Audrey puts on the dress she and her mother shopped for at Talbots over the Christmas break. It's pale pink fine-wale corduroy with a drop waist, a square neck, and a collar. She puts in pearl post earrings and fastens the string of pearls her parents gave her for high school graduation. She looks in the mirror and thinks about the fashion advice she read in a magazine: *Get dressed completely, then take off one piece of jewelry.* The neckline and collar show off her collarbone, which the pearls overshadow. That's what the article meant: *What you remove highlights what you keep.* She takes off the pearls and looks at herself from the side. Her roommate is down the hall getting help with her makeup, so Audrey has the room to herself. She puts the pearls back on and practices laughing and talking to the mirror.

Yes, it's been a great week! I've had so much fun! How are you? I loved your skit on Tuesday!

She takes them off and rehearses to her reflection again.

It's nice to see you again, too! The work St. Jude does is so important! I'm going to volunteer at a hospital this summer.

She is proud of her good clavicle. She traces it with her finger and smiles at the mirror. She is better off without the pearls, and the two in her ears, small as they are, do enough work.

Audrey warms up at the first party, at Pi Phi. She's relaxed, funny, and smart, and gets compliments on her dress. When she arrives at Tri Delt, she recognizes one of the girls she saw with Paxton before finals. She's standing by the table with punch and cookies on the far side of the room, talking to another girl Audrey has never seen before. There are so many members and rushees, Audrey hasn't seen either girl at the earlier parties. Paxton hadn't been friendly that night in the library, and Audrey was embarrassed by his reaction. She was only trying to act like what had happened had been one night of fun, something she could handle. Even if nothing else was going to happen with Paxton, she wanted him to like her, and she'd tried to act casual, *normal.* She just wanted to say hello to convey it had been no big deal. After that, having gotten the message, Audrey didn't bother him again. She tried to forget about it and move on.

The room is filled with chatter and nerves. Audrey walks to the table and picks up a glass of punch. She steps closer to the library girl and the one she's with.

"Oh, hello," says the library girl, scanning Audrey's name tag. "Audrey. This is Kira, and I'm Caitlin," says

Caitlin, indicating the other woman before sweeping her hand toward her own name tag. "I'm a senior, and Kira is a junior."

"Hello, Audrey," says Kira. She's wearing a black cashmere sweater set, a cream wool skirt, and a string of pearls. She twists them at her throat.

"Hi," says Audrey. "It's nice to meet you, Kira." She extends her hand, and Kira shakes it.

"It's nice to meet you, too, Caitlin," says Audrey. "I kind of met you in the library last semester?" Audrey waits for Caitlin to offer her hand, but she doesn't. Maybe, thinks Audrey, if Caitlin remembers her, too, there's no need for the formality. "You were talking to Paxton before finals?"

"Oh, did you?" Caitlin squints. "God, that was a lifetime ago. Kira is Paxton's girlfriend." Her open palm drifts toward Kira.

"How do you know Paxton?" says Kira.

Audrey's face reddens and her heart races and she can't think fast enough. *Act normal. It was no big deal. Settle down; you've met lots of other Tri Delts, and they liked you. You've made it this far.* "I just met him once at a party," she says. "He's a nice guy. You're lucky."

"Paxton met a lot of girls at a lot of parties last semester, I'm sure." Kira laughs. "I know how he is. For the poor girls who didn't keep their wits about them, well, that's the kiss, so to speak, of death."

Audrey bites her bottom lip with her top teeth. She holds her breath.

"I'm going to mingle a little," Caitlin said. "Work the room. Have fun."

"That's a really lovely dress," Kira says. "It's simple but lovely in its simplicity. I like that square neckline." She traces a square in the air between them with her index finger.

"Thank you," Audrey says. Her face is so hot. Talking to Paxton's girlfriend, she wants to rely on wit and charm — and the confidence she had at the earlier parties — but instead finds only panic in reserve. At least she has rehearsed.

"I really admire your sorority," says Audrey. "Everything about it. You just seem like a really great group of women. Your skit this week was so funny. I think the work of St. Jude is so important."

"Yeah, we have a good time," Kira says. "Why do you want to pledge, Audrey?"

"You know, I just really want to be part of something bigger, I guess," says Audrey. She wishes she had her own pearls to twist and worry. "A community of girls who are like me that has both fun and purpose. For friendship and mutual goals?" She thinks her words flounder in a way that they didn't in the other parties, where she hasn't cared as much. This conversation feels like an interview; none of the others had. "To do together whatever good we can. How about you? Why did you pledge?"

"It's so funny," says Kira, batting her hand at the air. "It wasn't even something I wanted. The Tri Delts wooed me. Looking back, I was in the right place at the right time. I just wasn't looking for it."

"Yeah." Audrey nods and smiles. She is on more solid ground. "Things work out that way sometimes."

"I will say," Kira says, "that for the Tri Delts, loyalty is our top priority. Everything else comes after that. Family first.

"Nice chatting with you, Audrey," says Kira. "You should talk to some other girls while you can. What time is it?" She glances at her watch. "Geez, this schedule is sheer madness. Twenty-five minutes, what's that? That's nothing. Go and visit with some sophomores. Have fun."

After Kira walks away, Audrey is relieved for the chance to talk to someone else, anyone else. As she scans for a pocket of girls she can join, she checks the direction Kira walked toward. She has crossed the room and is talking to Caitlin again. Their heads are bent toward each other, almost touching, and they are both staring at Audrey. Neither of them is smiling, but when Audrey catches their eyes, Caitlin lifts her hand in a passive wave. Audrey fears what's driving their stares — *We can see right through you* — but manages a wave back.

When the day's parties end and the girls get their bid cards, Audrey looks at the blank lines, ready for her top three choices, and doesn't think twice. She fills out the top one. *Delta Delta Delta.*

At seven o'clock on bid night the sisters collect their pledges. Audrey's roommate gets a bid from Pi Phi. Their RA comes and gets her. Audrey sits on the edge of her bed with her hands folded in her lap and looks at the floor.

She waits for a knock on the door. The hoots and screams of girls getting bids echo and bounce up and down the hallway. Their new sisters round them up and out of the building. The clock's digits click — 7:12, 7:13, 7:14.

Her eyes fill, and her throat tightens. She taps her foot and squeezes her folded hands. She unfolds her hands and over and over pinches and plucks the cream-and-blue toile of her bedspread. It's 7:23, then 7:24. Maybe someone will still knock, although the sounds of elation from the dorm grow faint as the girls leave the dorm and gather in the quad. Perhaps there has been a mistake, and tomorrow morning a Tri Delt will come and tell her they are so sorry; there was a terrible oversight the night before. A misunderstanding that confused all the sisters and filled them with remorse — each of them thinking someone else had collected her. Despite her desperate wish, she is gripped by grief at the knowledge that this isn't going to happen.

She needs something to hold and takes the pearls from her jewelry box. She sits back on her bed with the necklace, worrying each bead before caressing the next, her palms making them damp. She rocks and waits and frets and hopes while one harrowing image loops through her mind under its own power: Caitlin and Kira talking and staring at her, their expressions barely stifling their shared ridicule. She is way past the heartbreak inflicted by her fickle childhood best friend; well beyond the teenage shame of her older brother reading her diary, where she detailed, with naked honesty, her private adoration of his best friend. She has done something irreparably wrong. Yet trying to summon some comfort from what she holds, to believe in a simpler mistake than sleeping with the wrong guy, Audrey thinks: *Maybe I shouldn't have taken off the pearls.*

Paying the Piper

CAITLIN BUCKLEY—A strong and accomplished swimmer—is in the throes of her recurring dream, in which she is breathing under water when in an instant the skill abandons her and drowning is a certainty. Her agony melts into the real sound of retching, a sound that's coming from somewhere close. She bolts awake and squints at the clock. The red digits read 6:23 a.m.

She focuses in the dark and scans the room. She sees that Anne's bed is empty, her blankets flat. Disoriented and groggy, Caitlin staggers to her feet and feels her way out into the hall. Everyone else in the suite is asleep. She taps her fingernails on the bathroom door.

"Hey, are you okay?" she whispers.

"No," Anne says. "I'm pregnant. Goddamn it." She heaves between the words.

Caitlin slides down the wall and sits on the floor to wait

for her. What are the chances of this happening to both of them with Peter? This is her first thought, and then it's her only one.

Anne opens the door. She walks to their room, curled around herself, and burrows under her covers.

Caitlin follows her and sits on the edge of Anne's bed. She strokes a few stray locks of Anne's dark hair that are peeking out from under the blankets.

"Are you sure?" she says.

"I did three tests yesterday, all positive. You think maybe it was a bad lot?"

"How late are you?"

"Three weeks," Anne says. "Like, really, what else did I think it was going to be?"

"There's other stuff—it just never ends up being any of them," Caitlin says. "I'm sorry."

In the dark they stay this way for a while. Caitlin keeps smoothing Anne's hair and wonders if she's fallen back to sleep.

"Anne?"

"Yeah?" she mumbles.

"Do you want anything? Water or a soda? Do you feel like something to eat?"

"No, thanks, Buck."

"Okay," Caitlin says.

After a few seconds she whispers, "Why didn't you say anything?"

"Nothing to say till now."

Caitlin tucks a strand of Anne's hair under the blanket. "So I was going to get up and study, but I'll stay if you want me to. Do you want me to stay?" she asks.

"No," Anne says. "It's okay. I'm going to try and sleep."

"So we'll talk later, okay? Go get some coffee? A beer? Take a walk? You decide, okay? I'll find you later?"

"Yeah, okay. Thanks."

Caitlin gives Anne's blanketed arm a squeeze and gets off the bed.

She'll go with her if she wants her to. She'll do whatever Anne asks. Caitlin wonders if Peter will ask Anne to marry him and knows Anne would say no. Anne has plans, and marrying Peter isn't one of them. If Caitlin were Anne, she would say yes.

They're college seniors, and graduation is a few months away. Caitlin doesn't know what she's going to do, and people always want to know. They all ask the same question: "And what are you going to do?" Her parents, their friends, professors, other seniors, and underclassmen are interested and curious. She tells them she's still deciding, that there are just so many options out there. It's 1987 — they can do whatever they want and change their minds if one plan doesn't work. Maybe she'll apply to the Peace Corps, or stay and work in the admissions office. Make a professional career out of college life. Every day, for visiting high school seniors and their parents, be an example of the exceptional graduate their competitive Catholic university produces.

She'll be one, after all. She had desperately wanted to be a nun when she was eleven, which was accompanied by a phase of compulsive praying. Except for going to mass — regularly though infrequently, and more out of guilt than desire — attending a Jesuit university is the current demonstration of her devotion.

Anne knows what she's going to do, and Peter knows. Anne's gotten an incredible magazine internship, in Europe, no less, that will very likely turn into a big job. And Peter's been accepted to med school at Columbia. Anne has told Caitlin that Peter seems to think she might not take the job after the internship if it's offered because he's gotten into med school.

"He calls it the ticket," Anne said. "'Come with me to New York and you can do whatever you want,' he tells me — 'paint, draw, sculpt, whatever. Go to Parsons. We have *the ticket*.' Like one has anything at all to do with the other. The hell I'm not taking it if I get the job, which I most likely will. He could be going to the moon, but I'm not going to change my plans because of the fucking *ticket*. Christ, I'm *from* New York. Of course I'd rather go to Europe than back there."

She can never say the word *ticket* without doing air quotes and rolling her eyes, even in front of Peter. In response, if he's there, Peter grabs her around her waist or shoulder and pulls her into him. He laughs and leans over and kisses her and says, "Come on, Anne, we all know you're the real ticket."

*   *   *

Peter and Caitlin were in the same dorm freshman year. More than once they did laundry together in their building's basement. They never talked. While the machines made the room loud and hot, he never looked up from what he was reading as their clothes spun and rinsed and dried. He moved his awkward wet loads from one machine to the other and Caitlin sat nearby studying and breathing the same air he did. Then she got up and did the same thing while he sat. There had only been the two of them there, but they had both acted like they were alone.

In early April, Caitlin was walking back to the dorm after dinner and saw him juggling outside their limestone building. He was alone, deftly bouncing back and forth on his bare feet as he jockeyed to keep the balls in the air. He looked practiced at it, not like he was just learning, and Caitlin was captivated by how good he was. He was wearing shorts, a sweater, and a ski cap. That afternoon had been unseasonably hot, and pale coeds exposed their skin, unabashedly grateful for the sun's warmth, lying on blankets spread across the university's lawns. They wore shorts and tank tops, hoping for an early tan but getting burned instead. The chill that settled on the campus as the sun went down sent everyone back to warmer clothes.

Caitlin wanted to sit down and watch him juggle for as long as he was there, but she was shy, and the thought of him discovering her watching him was a powerful enough deterrent that she kept walking. Instead she went into their building and watched him through a window from a second-floor stairwell landing until it was so dark that he went inside. After he disappeared, she was disappointed and wished she'd been brave enough to say hello.

A few weeks later she went to a baseball game with several girls from her floor. One of them liked a guy on the team, so they all went to see him play. To Caitlin's surprise, Peter was the pitcher. She still didn't know his name, but he was the same guy from the laundry room. The reader and the juggler. It was easy to sit there and stare at him from behind her sunglasses — where else was she going to look until the ball was in play? He had the bill of his hat pulled down low, and she watched his left hand roll and massage the ball before every pitch. It was like the hand was thinking — taking its time and sleepily musing — about how best to let go and send the ball. The hand was separate from the person who was making the throw actually happen.

Peter shook off the catcher countless times during one player's at bat. So many, in fact, that the catcher finally walked out to the mound, looking defeated and pissed and lifting his mask as he marched. When he got there, Peter put his arm around the catcher's shoulder and all his lumpy gear, as though he were embracing an angry tortoise. Peter's mouth moved, and the catcher nodded, then trotted back to home plate. On the very next pitch, the batter hit a pop fly straight to center field, which the fielder caught, and the inning ended. Only then did Caitlin realize that there had been players on all three bases with two outs. Now that she had noticed him for the third time, she wanted to find out more about him. She didn't learn much that day, only that he had an older brother who was a senior and played varsity baseball. Their focus was the one girl and her questions about the crush boy: one of the floor mates who'd come along was in his Spanish class. There was a suspicion, with some uncertainty, that he was dating a sophomore. They were desperate to find out; it seemed so important.

After the baseball game Caitlin didn't see Peter again until senior week. She was a sorority pledge that semester, and the momentum of ceremonies and antics pulled her along while she balanced her classes with drinking contests and secret kidnappings. Her sorority Big Sister was graduating and had asked her to stay for senior week with her and her senior friends, who were all asking their little sisters to stay, too. It was a tradition in their chapter, and so after finals of course she stayed on.

Caitlin helped her freshman friends pack and load their parents' cars. She hugged them, said good-bye and have a great summer—you better write to *me!*—and waved and patted station-wagon tailgates before they drove off. They made up a kind of subculture, those who stayed behind after the end of classes and exams to lurk and linger until they had wrung the very last experiences out of the year.

That week, when they went into the first party, it was early, but groups of people were out and meeting up, getting the night under way. With no classes to attend or work to finish, the only thing to do was drink and play as early as there was a chance to. "Billie Jean" was pulsing from the speakers, but the dance floor was dark and empty when they arrived at the first house. Just beyond the dance floor, up a few stairs, the bar was well lit—garish—a moist, yeasty room emitting the stale smell of beer. There were two guys behind the bar pouring from the tap, and one of them was Peter. He had on a bowler hat and was smoking a cigar. The other guy was wearing a baseball cap backwards. Caitlin was surprised to see Peter at first, but she was an underclassman, too, and remembered he had a brother who was a senior.

She got in line to wait for a beer.

Peter looked across the bar and slid the wet cigar to the corner of his mouth and pointed his index finger at her.

"You're not graduating, are you?" he said.

The cigar in his mouth dangled, hinged between his lips. It hung, threatening to fall with each word he said. The smoke smelled dirty and reminded Caitlin of old men. They were the only people she'd ever known who smoked them.

"Are you?" she said.

"No, but my brother Matt is. My own flesh and blood. Wish Matt congratulations. He's going to be a doctor, aren't you, tiger?"

He pronounced *doctor* like "docta."

"There's a docta in the house!" Peter said. "Your parents must be so proud."

He put his arm around the baseball-hat guy, who patted

Peter on the head with his free hand, the one not being squeezed in the embrace.

"Congratulations, Matt," Caitlin said.

"Thanks," Matt said. "And I offer you my condolences. Tonight, consider yourself a potential witness." He pulled the bowler hat down over Peter's eyes. "This is Peter," he said. "The baby of the family."

"I'm Caitlin."

"Well, *are* you, Caitlin?" Peter stabbed the air between them with his finger again. He shoved Matt away and pushed the bowler far back on his head.

"Am I what?" she said.

"Uh, hello, *graduating?*" he said, lengthening the word and holding his hands out wide in front of him as though she didn't understand English.

"No. We were in the same dorm this year. I'm a freshman, too."

"Well, that's good news," he said. "Hey, want to play pool?"

That was the start of her week with Peter. That night they drank and played pool and darts and served people beer and deejayed. They were all over the place.

Well past midnight, Caitlin was in a bright stairwell, talking to a girl from her pledge class. She could see Peter in the dark hallway a few feet away. He was leaning against the paneled wall as though he were sleeping standing up. His head was tilted so that his profile and the brim of the bowler hat both pointed at the ceiling.

Because it was so hot that night, she'd worn a pale ivory sundress with eyelets stitched into the fabric. It was too nice a dress for fraternity parties, but because she loved it and because of the heat, she didn't care. Her friend left, and Caitlin walked into the hall and leaned against the wall next to Peter. Their arms and hands formed two touching parallel lines, skin on skin. In spite of the heat, he felt cool against her, and the hard angles of his knuckles grazed hers.

"Did you get a little nap in?" she said.

"Caitlin."

"Yeah?" she said.

He was quiet.

"What is it? Are you okay?"

"Of course. You know what? Caitlin. Do you know what?"

She was drunk. "I have no idea. What, Peter?"

"You know I could see right through your dress when you were over there talking."

She felt such a rush of heat right then, a current coursing through her. It seemed like everything that was about to happen was already done and being recalled fondly years later. Nothing about Peter seemed like a bad idea.

"I liked it. I really liked what I saw." He pivoted, rolling his left shoulder along the wall, and folded his length and weight over and onto her. He took both her hands in his and opened his mouth over hers and pushed her up against the wood paneling. He guided her right hand down to his pants. They ended up back in her room, and in the hot quiet they were at it before Caitlin could even get the dress off. The hours floated by until the sun was creeping up after the chirping of the earliest birds. As soon as they woke up he rolled on top of her and was inside her again.

Afterward he pulled on his jeans and sneakers and draped his T-shirt over his shoulder. "You come find me tonight, Caitlin, okay?" He straddled her, on his knees, his shirt hanging like a curtain, floating in front of her face. He kissed her and squeezed her naked ass with both his hands. His juggling hands, his pitching hands. She expected him to take off his pants and they'd go again, but he didn't. "I'll be looking for you."

And so every night passed like that the whole week, her first college spring. The second night they both smoked cigars, a pipe, a few cigarettes, cloves, too, and some weed from a bong a fraternity brother of his had. Caitlin tried chew and wore the bowler hat. Peter carried her piggyback from party to party. When they got back to her room she wore the sundress again when he asked her to put it on. The third night it rained, and they had sex on the wet lawn down between a knoll and their dorm. That's where the smell of wet grass in May still takes her.

He tried to teach her how to juggle. They walked out to the baseball field, stopping to make out along the way. He laid her down in the infield and spread her legs apart below the inky sky where he'd pitched just weeks before. Peter brushed her hair from her face and held both sides of her

jaw in his hands while he kissed her. By their last night together Caitlin thought she loved him. She felt like a rock
he'd taken and carved something out of. She was a different
person from the one she'd been a week ago.

After their last night together he left her room before
seven. The morning was already hot, and they had slept
without a sheet or blanket. He lifted her hair and kissed the
back of her neck.

"You have a great summer, Caitlin." He pulled her skin
into his mouth and slapped her bare behind. "I'll see you
next year."

She lay in bed after he left, replaying his words. She felt
stupid, expecting him to have said something different,
something about being in touch over the summer, but
maybe, she thought, he would — he just hadn't thought that
far ahead.

She was exhausted when she got home, and she stayed
exhausted. She and Tracy, her best friend from high school,
had gotten hired at a local nursery, and it was backbreaking
and dull work from the get-go. The potting shed was a humid, stifling wall of steaming soil. The junipers were in-
tractable and temperamentally prickly foes, leaving small
but excruciating scratches like mild purgatories on their
hands, which threatened to never heal. She imagined Peter
throughout the boredom of her days, at home with his own
family and friends in a city she'd never seen. He was paint-
ing houses and doing landscape jobs all summer before
going to the shore for the month of August with his family.

His two older brothers had done the same summer job for years, too.

"My family knows a guy," he'd told her one night during their week together. "We've always known him, and we've always worked for him." His family knew the guy going way back, and there was a lot of work, so much work. From early in the day until the sky's light was gone, from May until August. They always made bank over the summer and got strong, tan backs and smooth, flat stomachs out of the deal.

After two weeks at the nursery, she was still fatigued, and her breasts were swollen and tender. Wearing a bra hurt, and not wearing one hurt worse. While Caitlin waited for her period, thinking every day *Maybe today I will bleed,* she already knew she wasn't going to. She thought back to May. She thought she had finished her period right before senior week, and there had been no mention or appearance of condoms. Maybe she'd gotten the dates wrong. Or maybe her usual cycle had betrayed her body. It was too late to speculate.

Caitlin and Tracy went to the drugstore and then to the swim club one Sunday morning after mass. In the bathroom's large stall she peed on the stick and asked Tracy to watch it for her.

After the elapsed time Caitlin said, "Throw it away."

"Don't you want to know?" Tracy said.

"I already do."

"I'm sorry. Caitlin, what are you going to do?"

"What do you think?" She started to cry.

Tracy touched Caitlin's hair and put her arm around her. "Do you need money? I have some saved, and it's yours if you want it."

"I might." Caitlin leaned into her. "I'll let you know."

"Cait, who was it?"

Tracy was the only one she ever told, the only one who'd ever known about her and Peter. Caitlin scheduled an abortion for the next Friday, and Tracy drove her. The girls took the day off, and Tracy stayed with her until they took Caitlin back and asked her all the questions to make sure she was sure and gave her Valium and explained about the scraping and the suctioning and exactly how long it would take and the bleeding and the cramping and the clots afterward. And they were right: everything they told her they'd do and everything they said would happen turned out exactly as they had said it would. Caitlin squeezed the nurse's hand the whole time and pressed her eyes shut and prayed *I'm sorry, I'm sorry, I'm sorry, please, please, please* until it was over. The Valium could only do so much.

Afterward they went to the movies. *Against All Odds* was playing that summer, and Caitlin sobbed in the dark, chilly theater, not feeling out of place because it was a cavernous hull of a space and besides, who cared? Also, although it was the middle of the afternoon and the theater wasn't very full, she could hear other moviegoers crying, too. Tracy kept her right arm around her for the whole movie, and her left hand held Caitlin's left hand. She let go of Caitlin only to hand her tissues while that Phil Collins song played forever — *Take a look at me now* — and Caitlin wept until she couldn't cry anymore. Later she imagined the audience was all just a bunch of girls who'd taken the day off to have an abortion. It was such a bad movie, and who saw a crappy movie in the middle of the day during the summer, anyway?

Tracy dropped her off at home late that afternoon. She put the car in park and rested her hand on Caitlin's arm. "You know you did the right thing," she said. Tracy squeezed her arm. "I know that doesn't make it any better, but I really think you did."

Caitlin opened the car's passenger door and pressed her foot against the right angle of the curb. She looked down at her hands in her lap, as though they held an answer waiting to be recognized. "Don't ever let it happen to you," she said.

She quietly improved. She and Tracy got tan, and Caitlin felt looked after by her all summer as they got better at the job and brought pots of free roses home for their mothers and coached their fathers about using ground cover to make their yards more interesting and dimensional. They saved money and shopped at Goodwill for other people's castoffs they thought were cool. Caitlin started running and biking and swimming, and although she had gotten a prescription for birth control pills, she didn't fill it. She had sworn off boys for the time being. She planned to go to confession but kept putting it off, Saturday after Saturday. How could she begin to tell a priest any of it? It would be a little like showing up in a foreign country one day, not knowing how to speak the language, and asking a stranger for help with a secret family recipe, wouldn't it?

In July her mother suggested she finally unpack the boxes she hadn't touched. "Go through those relics from your freshman year, sweetie, and make room for next year's," she said. "Get rid of what you don't want."

When Caitlin imagined returning to campus, she buckled under pangs of alarm. She had looked up Peter's address in the campus directory. Nothing about that week seemed real now. What was she going to do, call him? Reach out from another area code and say, *Hi, remember me? Guess what? And how's your summer going?* Get him a Hallmark card and write Lionel Richie lyrics on it and drop it in the mail? *Hello.* He hadn't called or written. Caitlin told herself what had happened happened, but it hadn't meant anything; it was just biology. She had wanted him, God, she had wanted him so badly. Peter and his perfect arms and dimples and crafty glances and his hands, with their ropy veins, intertwined with her fingers. She'd wanted him and his bowler hat. She wanted, even for just a week, to latch onto his extraordinary ability to do anything easily. To have him bring her along with him as he glided through the world and the world got out of his way.

And he had wanted Caitlin, too. Every night he had. To track her down if she didn't find him first and to smack her on the ass and to push her dress up over her hips and pull her on top of him and fuck her up against the wall and to parade around the university campus in the dark with her for a week, but that was it. He'd never even looked up and said hi when they'd done laundry. What Caitlin never told Tracy was that she had already been heartbroken, ashamed by the pregnancy, ashamed of loving the thrill of what got her pregnant. Her effect on Peter, his being so attentive for a week, had been powerful and heady. She couldn't endure the possible heartbreak of his rejecting her now, even if telling him might turn out better than she imagined. What could he say or do? Be her boyfriend? Pay half? She couldn't take the risk. Nothing else was going to happen, because Caitlin had decided. He didn't owe her something in lieu of what she hadn't given herself. She'd been stupid, but she wouldn't be again.

She returned to school at the end of August. Driving past the Philadelphia exits—almost there—she was more nervous than she'd been as a freshman and wished she hadn't eaten breakfast. A flurry of thousands of students descended on the university. Caitlin set up her room with a new roommate, Liz, one of her pledge sisters. They used double-sided tape to hang posters of Monet's water-lily paintings and Tom Cruise in *Risky Business* on their yellow cinder-block walls and bought fetching adhesive paper to line their drawers. They organized their cassettes and wrote their initials on the tapes—the Police, R.E.M., Madonna, Genesis, Billy Joel— with a black Sharpie. Caitlin joined committees in the sorority. She ran and swam. She went to the library some nights on the weekends or went to the movies and stayed out of the fraternities. She traveled in a pack of sorority sisters. She felt a little like a spy or a mobster, always discreetly scanning the crowd for Peter. She spotted him several times across the dining hall and from afar, walking on campus. Every time she saw him, she occupied herself in conversation or changed direction. Whatever she could to maintain the distance between them.

Toward the end of the first semester, right before finals in December, when Christmas decorations and music were omnipresent on campus from one end to the other, as Caitlin walked into the campus bookstore, Peter passed her walking out.

"Hey, hey, Caitlin." He grabbed her arm and petted it through her wool winter coat. He ran his other hand through his hair. "I haven't seen you out at all this year. How've you been? Wow, you look really great," he said. "I thought I'd run into you before now."

He let go of her and folded his arms across his chest. He stared down at Caitlin and rocked on his heels, expectant. His hair was longer, shaggier than it had been in the spring. A pimple on the left side of his nose shamelessly sported a dominating white head. Still, the way he talked and stared made Caitlin's stomach flip and surge.

"I'm good," she said. "I'm great. Busy, you know. Studying. Getting ready for the holidays. I'm going in to shop right now. Merry Christmas." She walked away and left him standing there.

"Yeah, merry Christmas to you, too," he said to her re-treating back.

She raced into the store and disappeared down one of the textbook aisles and breathed and waited. She couldn't stand there and have a simple conversation. She didn't trust herself. Part of her wanted to, but it was beyond her. She wanted to flirt and pick up where they'd left off in the spring, but she didn't know how to play that role. Instead she was certain she would start crying or blurt out regret-table words before she could stop them. The pull to repeat their brief history tapped her guilt along with it. Now that she had finally run into him, she told herself, the next time would be better. It wouldn't be the first time, and she would be better, too. She was confident it would be no worse.

And she was right. Caitlin did see him during the next semester at games and once at a crowded party after she finally started going to them again, and it was okay. She was aloof and distant toward him, maybe even cold. She didn't mean to be unfriendly, but she intentionally avoided being near him or making eye contact, and any exchanges she had with him during that time were brief and superficial. She fell for other boys that year and slept with them, never without a condom, and they weren't ever as important as anything else she was doing and nothing with them was ever as powerful as the week she had spent with Peter.

In the beginning of her junior year, the girl from her freshman floor who'd dragged them all to the baseball game that day told her that the player she was interested in—

whom she still, sadly, liked, unrequited — and another guy on the team, Peter Herring, had gone abroad for the year. Caitlin was liberated. There was no chance of seeing him. She basked in the gift of comfort and relief that there was no preparation or rehearsal or surveillance necessary to get through a day, a night, or the whole rest of the school year.

Anne Cavanaugh has been Caitlin's dearest friend since they were sophomores. They met in January of that year, when everything from Caitlin's freshman year was like a shadow that trailed her but paled with every step she took forward.

They were in a drawing class together, and on the first day Anne picked the easel next to Caitlin's. She took off her coat and put down her backpack. "So do you think this is going to be worth it?" she said.

"What do you mean?" Caitlin said.

"Well, this isn't an art school, so I just hope I get something out of it. I'm Anne."

"I'm Caitlin," she said. "I guess it will be better than the class at the community center, but beyond that who knows?"

"Right." She laughed and sat down. "Good point."

"I'm not very artistic," said Caitlin, "so I might not even be able to tell you if it's worth it."

"I'll let you know," Anne said. She tucked a dark curl behind her ear and bent over to unpack her supplies.

"How come you didn't go to art school?" Caitlin said.

"Parents." Anne shrugged, as though that covered it all. "So we all agreed. Here I am now, and they'll compromise later."

They hit it off that day from the very start, as though they'd been friends in past lives. Their friendship developed in an easy, steady way. Anne encouraged her to do radical, instinctive things with line and composition because Caitlin was self-conscious. Anne said helping her made her own work better. Sometimes they went to the studio at night, and Anne would have Caitlin sketch with her eyes closed. Anne started swimming with Caitlin because she had never even learned the crawl. "I can play in a pool or the ocean for hours," Anne joked. "But for me swimming means the dog paddle or simply staying alive in the water."

Within the first month of meeting, they'd become almost inseparable. One night that spring Anne wanted to go out, but Caitlin had a cold and decided to stay in. She was in bed, and Anne was sitting at the end of it, her back against the wall. Her bent knees made a triangle over Caitlin's blanketed feet.

"I know you're not feeling well, but it's a bummer for me."

"You don't need me," Caitlin said. "Go out with Liz, Steph, Meghan, and those guys. They're a blast."

"Yeah, I will, I guess." she said. "You know, you just make nights out better, Buck. I'm more fun when I'm out with you. People don't think I'm so serious when we're together."

They were in different sororities, but there was a kind of

cross-pollination between their sisterhoods. With the over-
lap, six of them—three from one sorority and three from
the other—became a social force to be reckoned with.
They went out in a group on the weekends, blanketing
whichever party they went to, drinking, the circle of them
dancing like crazy to their favorite songs, hooking up or
saving each other from hooking up, getting home in the
wee hours, and going over it all the next morning, hung-
over, at breakfast. They made Caitlin feel insulated and
omnipotent.

One night during midterms, Caitlin stayed up with Anne
while she worked on an art history paper. They were
camped out in the lounge of Anne's dorm, and when she
finished writing out each page in longhand, she handed it
to Caitlin to type. It was late when they were finally done,
and when Caitlin got back to her room she saw that Liz
had left a note for her on the dry-erase board—*Using the
room, k?*—which meant her boyfriend was staying over. It
was shitty, but it was so late she guessed Liz thought she
wasn't coming home. She walked back to Anne's building.
She found a door propped open, climbed the three flights
of stairs, and tapped on her door.

"Hey, it's me again."

Anne emerged from the darkness and squinted into the
bright hallway. "What's up?"

"Can I crash here?" Caitlin said. "Eric's in our room. I just
need a blanket and the floor."

Anne's roommate was already asleep.

"Sure. But the floor's no good," she whispered. "We can both sleep in my bed. Like a couple of shoes. Shoeing instead of spooning." Anne giggled. They climbed in and arranged themselves — head to toe — in her single bed.

Caitlin was almost asleep and almost didn't hear Anne. "Thanks for your help with that paper. You saved my ass. I love you, Buck." A friend had never said that to her before, and she had never said it, either.

"I love you too, Anne."

Then they slept like a pair, together for the rest of that short night.

Whenever they were partying and drinking and smoking pot or doing mushrooms, she was tempted to tell Anne about Peter and her abortion, and she came close one night when Anne told her that she almost went to the hospital freshman year for overdrinking.

They were walking to the all-night convenience store near campus after being out — starving and somewhere between drunk and sober. The rest of the girls had all gone to bed.

"I'm glad I'm not anywhere close to the kind of mess I was last year," Anne said. She linked her arm through Caitlin's. "If I'd killed myself, we never would have met."

"What the hell are you talking about?" said Caitlin. She stopped walking. "You almost killed yourself? I'm just hearing this now?"

"No, come on," Anne said, her elbow pulling at Caitlin's where they hinged. "No, nothing like that. Last year I got so drunk my friends wanted me to go to the hospital. I was falling all over the place. I don't remember. We had this punch, our floor and the boys' floor below us had this party, and I don't even know what was in it or how much I had. I went to bed and puked in my sleep. I guess that's what happened. That's what I woke up to anyway. All over. My hair and everything. I dodged a bullet."

"Jesus," said Caitlin. "That's scary."

"I considered it a free pass," Anne said. "No repeats for me on that."

They got to the store, bought chili dogs, and ate them on the walk back.

After what Anne had shared, Caitlin felt the urge to confess something in return. Although they were all drinking, and occasionally having sex, the abortion was a dark and shameful part of her, not party talk. And her grief felt ancient, farther in the past than nine months ago. Spilling her story now seemed to have little point and no upside. She felt like the only reason to say something was to unload the remaining weight of her recklessness — with a boy she barely knew but had wanted so badly — a recklessness that tenaciously clung to her, that she still couldn't entirely shake. But she knew that no matter how much she'd already talked to Tracy, nothing she'd said to her or could say to anyone else would loosen that load, break it up, and make it disappear completely. She locked away the temptation to say anything more to anyone. Now she was done with it. She conceded that her mistake was a part of her she would never be wholly rid of. Made some sacred space within and buried all of it. Both what could have been and what was.

Rather than confess, Caitlin played it safe. "I'm glad you told me, and I'm glad you were okay. We'll keep an eye on each other. Make sure nothing like that happens again to either of us."

"Deal," said Anne.

The compromise on Anne's parents' part was that she could spend her junior year in Italy. Caitlin already knew, early in the friendship, how important it was for her to go. Anne's year away was always part of who she was, so Caitlin never felt resentful that they'd spend that time apart.

In June, a month after their sophomore year ended, a TWA flight was hijacked en route from Greece to Rome — the Rome airport was the same one Anne would be flying into in a few months. Caitlin had gotten a job in an upscale gourmet deli that summer and heard the report on the radio at work. She called Anne as soon as she got home.

"Are you still going?" she asked her. "Aren't you scared?"

"Now's the time *to* go," Anne said. "Right after something like this happens, everyone else is a lot safer. It's terrible for the people it happened to, but a hijacking won't happen again there. I'll be fine."

The story remained in the news for weeks, until the hostages were released, but not before a US Navy diver had been murdered and thrown out of the plane onto the tarmac in Beirut, an image that was aired excessively, Caitlin thought. The people who loved him didn't need to see that over and over.

Caitlin went to visit Anne for a week that summer, after the ordeal was over. Anne's family lived on the Upper East Side, in a building that had a doorman who nodded and tipped his hat as they came and went. They talked about it, and Caitlin told Anne that even if she wasn't scared, it didn't matter. That Anne going to a part of the world where terrorism could happen made her feel out of control, and that she couldn't count on Anne being safe.

"I don't know what I'd do if something happened to you," Caitlin said. "I just can't even imagine how I'd be able to live. Experts say people who lose a friend when they're young are never the same again." They had gone running around the reservoir in Central Park and were walking to cool down.

"I know," Anne said. "I guess I'd be feeling the same way if you were going and I was staying. It's not that I'm not nervous — I am — but I'm not scared, not scared enough, you know? To not go, I mean."

Clutching her sweaty Walkman, Caitlin felt too young, too out of her league, to be having this conversation. It was like playing pretend, playing grown-up. She wanted Anne's parents to forbid her from going and make her stay at school for the next year.

"You know, Caitlin," Anne said, "I just think whatever happens is supposed to. What if I stayed here and was in a car accident and died? Then we'd be thinking, 'That wouldn't have happened if she'd been in Italy.'"

"Well *I* would," said Caitlin. "That's exactly what I'd be thinking and saying to everyone while I was mourning you. I don't think you'd be thinking anything."

Anne laughed. "Yes, I would, too. I'd be missing you like hell from the afterlife and keeping an eye on you. Helping keep your ass safe."

The first piece of mail Caitlin got that year was Anne's postcard of the Trevi Fountain.

dear buck! i love it here! it could only be better if you were here too. i am safe and sound—do not you worry! more soon! much love! here's my address.—a

Caitlin was busy that year. She reviewed movies and books for the school paper, which turned into a regular column, and she was secretary of her sorority. She sent Anne a postcard with a picture of the campus.

I like your backyard better than mine! Have so much fun for the both of us but you better come back! Stay safe, miss you tons! Love, Buck xo

In early October, she heard from Anne again.

dearest buck, how strange to come to italy only to end up dating a boy from school! i've met this guy—he's smart and handsome and super funny, kind of a joker really.

half the time he doesn't seem to take anything seriously so I'm surprised he even applied for this program. but since i've gotten to know him i've found out he's really into it and we're having fun. he's premed but he's an italian minor. we'll see how long this lasts! i'm not going to hold my breath! how is school? write okay? i miss you, a little homesick....much love! —a

Caitlin wrote back just before midterms.

I'm in the middle of an all-nighter and had to take a break, I can barely see straight. You go to Italy and get a local boyfriend? That's crazy! (For you, not him!) What about all those hot Italians?! Love you! —Cait

After that, months lapsed without any word from Anne. It wasn't until close to Christmas that she heard from her again. Caitlin had written to her in November. Just before she left for the break she got a Christmas card from her.

dear buck, so sorry i haven't written in so long! how are you? i hope school is good this year, i'm sure you're busy too. your column sounds great, will you send me one? italy is great and i can't believe it's already half over! some days i still miss school though so i'm sure i'll be ready to come back. i'm going home for half the break and to pittsburgh for the other half but I'll try to call you during vacation if we don't get a chance to see each other. ti amo!—a

Anne didn't say anything about the boy she'd met. Pittsburgh? Caitlin forgot this detail as soon as she finished the note. Maybe Anne had relatives there that she'd never mentioned, and her whole family was going to visit grandparents and cousins they hadn't seen in years.

On Christmas Eve Caitlin went to a party at a high school friend's with Tracy. She helped her family host Christmas dinner. Her grandmother, aunts, uncles, and cousins all came, ate, and left, as they did every year.

Three days later, her mother woke her early. "Sweetie," she said. "I'm sorry. But I think you should see this."

The newspaper's headline about the terrorist attack that morning at the Leonardo da Vinci airport in Rome shocked Caitlin awake. Two Americans had been killed—one was a male college student whose name she didn't recognize. She felt like she was going to be sick.

She left her bed, sprinted down the stairs, and called Anne, waking her, too. Anne was fine; she'd gotten home on December 20. She was sorry she hadn't called; there had been a lot going on. She was shocked by the news and was sorry Caitlin had worried. Anne was shaken, too, Caitlin could tell. Anne kept saying how safe things were the day she flew out, how uneventful the flight was. How calm things had been throughout the whole fall. She didn't know the student who had been killed. He hadn't been in her program. They imagined how horrible it must have been. How the victims' families and friends were certainly reeling. Caitlin was grateful she wasn't one of them and felt guilty that she was grateful.

"I'm sorry we haven't talked till now," Anne said. "I'm sorry it's because of this. I've been wanting to call you. My mom found a lump in her breast and had a mastectomy a month ago. She's fine. She's doing chemo, and they got it all. Can you believe she didn't even tell me about it until I got home? She didn't want me to be worried."

"Are you?" Caitlin asked. One of the things she loved about Anne was that nothing seemed to faze her. This, apparently, was a trait she had inherited from her mother.

"Not really," Anne said. "Since she's not. She's pissed about losing her hair, though. So she's indulging in Hermès to make up for it. Merry fucking Christmas."

"Will you tell her hi?" Caitlin said. "Let her know I'm thinking of her."

After forty-five minutes of such a heavy call they were both wrung out. They said they'd talk again during the break.

"Don't worry, Buck. I'll be okay," Anne said.

"Just be careful, Anne. Take care of yourself. Love you."

"I love you, too."

After the break, on a morning in late January, Caitlin passed a crowd of people gathered in front of the television in the student union's basement. She had just done badly on a quiz that she should have aced, or she would have stopped. But she was depressed and frustrated and wanted to hide and take a nap.

When she got to her suite, all her suite mates and some of their neighbors were crowded around the TV in their lounge, too. The *Challenger* space shuttle had exploded right after takeoff, and people were glued to the reports. Caitlin watched for a while, then went to her room and tried to sleep. It was too overwhelming to stay and hear the tragedy and speculations recounted over and over. She really missed Anne, but the combination of the quiz and the space shuttle and the scare she'd had about her over Christmas all made Caitlin wish she was with her so she had something good to lean on. They hadn't been in touch over the holiday again after all. Caitlin imagined Anne's family and her mother's cancer had dominated her visit. She couldn't sleep, so she got out the airmail stationery she had bought for Anne's year away and sat on her bed.

Dear Anne, My God what a terrible day. Have you heard about the Challenger? It just happened and it's all over the TV, on all the channels and everyone is talking about it. I just sucked on a quiz in Professor Reed's class and I was so bummed out about it, which seems stupid now, since the shuttle. They keep showing the outside of the school where the teacher worked and it's so sad and awful I couldn't watch anymore. I hope you're safe and happy since you've gone back. The girls all went skiing over the break and it was awesome. Wish you'd been there. How is your mom? I really miss you terribly, especially today. Love you! Caitlin

The semester was well under way before she heard from Anne again. Just before spring break, the phone in Caitlin's suite rang one afternoon when she was studying for midterms. She answered it, and laughter came over the delayed connection.

"Caitlin!" Anne screamed. "You're there! It's me!"

"Hi!" she screamed back. "How are you? Where are you?"

Anne giggled, and Caitlin clung to every detail that traveled through the tenuous line between them.

"We're out right now and we're pretty drunk and I told PJ I have to call my friend, damn it, and he said okay but good luck she probably won't be there and I said oh yes she will and I was right! You are there, of course you are!"

"What time is it there? Is it hot?"

"Buck! What time? Oh, it's, what time is it?" Caitlin heard Anne ask someone.

Anne came back. "It's, like, midnight, I think. Oh, it's so great. I wish you and all the girls could come visit for spring break. Could you imagine? It is really fabulous, and I love it so, and I'll be home in a few months! I'll be back for senior year! But you know what? I'm coming back here again, too, that's for sure. Maybe you can come with me then. Oh, I have to go—can you hear that beep? Shit; our time's almost up. I wish we had longer. I'll write to you soon!"

"Bye, Anne!" said Caitlin. "I'll write, too!" But she wasn't sure if Anne was still there or if she was talking to dead air.

In April, she got Anne's next letter.

dear caitlin! i was so happy to talk to you that night—that was a crazy one! i miss you too but i am having such a wonderful time and it's so hard to explain in a letter or call. i hope you've been having a mostly great year (Reed is a hardass just for the sake of it, you know that!) anyway everything we're seeing and doing and studying is amazing and makes me feel like our country is so young, so small, but i have to tell you this other thing that's happened. i've fallen in love—that's probably ridiculous to read, i know, don't think i'm crazy! but i have and you'll love him too, i know you will and then you'll see what i mean. remember the guy i told you about when i first got here? well it's really turned into something serious if you can believe it. pj—his name is peter jude herring, don't you just love it!—he's from school but i never met him before this program. i'm not surprised, campus is so huge, but to not meet there and meet all the way over here is too ironic! anyway, he is just, well i don't even know how to tell you. he makes me feel a way i've never felt before. he's just a fantastic guy and a great kisser and in bed…but when we go to the movies or lectures and hold hands, he folds both of his around mine, like he's carrying a baby bird.

Caitlin stopped reading. Peter was the guy? How was it him? She dug into her memory. He was abroad, too. *He* lived in Pittsburgh. By the time she got this letter, the boy Anne had talked about had blossomed in Caitlin's mind, briefly and months ago, into an imaginary person. No one she'd ever known or met. Fueled by her shock, she unraveled the idea of that made-up boy and reconciled the two people—the person. Peter, whom Anne had met in Italy and loved, and Peter. Her Peter.

She imagined Anne falling for him in the same way and for the same reasons Caitlin had, but with more time, at a different time. What couple ever says, "Well, we knew each other for a week and fucked more than we talked and had a pregnancy she aborted but we knew we were meant to be from the beginning and next year is our fortieth wedding anniversary"? No one, that's who. It never would have worked for Peter and her. She told herself that.

As stunned as Caitlin was, she was grateful for the months she had to prepare before they came back to school together as a couple. When she stopped thinking about Anne's revelation and herself on one side of Anne's life, she wondered about the other side. What had Anne told Peter about her? What had he said to Anne?

For their senior year, Caitlin had drawn lots on behalf of herself and Anne and gotten them housing in the elite suite complex that Caitlin had lived in as a junior. They talked on the phone a few weeks before school started and arranged to arrive on the same day at around the same time. Anne said she couldn't wait to see Caitlin. Caitlin said she couldn't wait, either.

When she got to campus, some of their other suite mates were already moving in, and Caitlin grabbed a coffee before she started unpacking her car. By the time she finished the coffee and had unloaded almost all her stuff, Anne and Peter drove up. Caitlin was sitting on the floor in their room, by the window, and Anne's voice soared up and through it when they got out of the car.

"Buck's here already!" she yelled.

She heard Anne fly up the outside stairwell. Anne launched herself into the suite as Caitlin walked out of their room. When Anne saw her she screamed and came at Caitlin with her arms out. Until this point Caitlin had been nervous, unsure of what this would be like because of Peter and not seeing Anne for a whole year. But in that instant she was relieved and elated that Anne was back.

Anne clutched her tightly. "Oh, Buck! I'm so, so, so happy to see you! Can you believe how long it's been!" She was breathless, and her words tumbled out on top of each other.

"I'm so glad to see you, too!" Caitlin said. "I love your hair!" Anne had cut her dark, shoulder-length hair, and it was short, like Twiggy's famous pixie style. She was beautiful and looked, Caitlin thought, European.

"You're so skinny!" Anne chimed. During Anne's time away, Caitlin had turned into a runner, a dedicated athlete.

They were still fussing over each other when Peter

walked up the stairs and leaned in the doorway. He just watched them while they both talked at the same time, interrupting each other, trying to catch up on every detail at once and share their year apart first thing.

Anne finally turned to him. "Will you come and say hi to Caitlin?"

He walked over, put his arm around Anne's shoulder, and grinned at Caitlin.

"Hey, Caitlin, how's it going?"

"Hi, Peter, welcome back."

"Is your car unloaded?" he said.

"Pretty much, but I can help you guys. Anne, how's your mom?"

"She's great, done with chemo, and her hair is growing back," said Anne.

"I'm so glad," Caitlin said. "That's great news."

"Sorry—I have to go see the room!" Anne chirped. It was like she'd never left.

Peter walked downstairs to Anne's car, and Anne skipped into the bedroom. Left alone and given the choice of whom to follow, Caitlin trailed Peter down to the street. He was lifting boxes out of Anne's trunk and putting them on the sidewalk.

"What can I take?" she said.

When he stood up from under the trunk's lid, she realized it was the first time they'd been alone since meeting outside the bookstore. His hair was very short. He looked like he had spent the last month on the beach. As tall as he'd always been. Caitlin regretted not going with Anne instead.

Peter rested against Anne's car and looked toward the suite complex before his gaze settled on Caitlin. He folded his arms across his chest, as though he had all the time in the world.

"How are you, Caitlin?" he said. "How was your junior year?"

"Not bad," she said.

"You know, I'm not a dick. An idiot sometimes, but not a dick," he said. "I'm sorry if I did something that made you think I was."

She wasn't expecting this. "Okay."

"I'm not. I just wanted to make sure you knew that."

"I'm sorry, Peter. I really don't know what to say." She felt in over her head alone with him. She hadn't thought she would.

He smiled at her. "A few years ago, you treated me like I was a bad guy."

"That was a long time ago," she said. She picked up a box from the sidewalk and held it between them.

"No, not so long," he said. "A little over two years."

"Well, I'm the one who's sorry, then," she said. "I didn't think that, and I don't. Really, it's cool."

"Okay," he said, and smiled at her again. "I didn't want you to worry about Anne. Anne with a bad guy."

"So I won't."

"Thanks, Caitlin."

She looked down and away from him and took the box up to the suite.

After they unpacked her car, Anne and Peter went to see other people and to Peter's apartment off campus. They planned to meet up later for beers, and Caitlin decided to go for a run first. She was rattled by what Peter had said. She would never have guessed that he cared enough to say something. She couldn't tell, and had no way to know for sure, if he had really liked her so much—he could have looked her up in the campus directory and found her during sophomore year, before or after they ran into each other prior to Christmas, and he hadn't—or if it was just the first time a girl had ever slammed a door on him.

She shouldn't have worried so much about what to do and how to act. Nothing has ever come up between her and Anne about Peter, it just hasn't, and they've all settled into their routines. But she does feel like she's lost Anne to him—their priority is being alone together virtually all the time—and Caitlin has to remind herself sometimes that it's not the previous year. She hardly ever sees Anne, just coming and going, sometimes for a few days on end and then not for a while. Out at parties. Notes exchanged on the dry-erase board. It's the price girls pay all the time in exchange for a boy—they let their friendships atrophy and fall by the wayside, suspend them, until they need them again. Maybe she would be exactly the same way, wanting as much as she could get from a boy she loved, as long as she could, knowing friends will wait and forgive.

Anne spends most nights at Peter's apartment, which suits her fine. Caitlin thinks there's something funny about each of them having been in bed together at one time or another. Caitlin and Peter. Then Caitlin and Anne. They hadn't lain like lovers that night—or been lovers, of course—but they'd slept as close. Now Anne and Peter.

Caitlin's thinking *I had him first* gives her hollow comfort, but she thinks it anyway, without meaning to. And more nights than she'd like to admit, by herself in the dark, she replays sleeping with him. On her back, sometimes on her stomach. Anne does the same things with him now that Caitlin did then. She is quiet. Although she's alone, there are three other doubles that comprise the suite. Sometimes masturbating helps, but other times it really doesn't, and she takes breaks in between. Finds a boy at a party to bring home and fuck.

Knowing Anne is pregnant, Caitlin is preoccupied all day. She can't study. She can only go through the motions and think about meeting Anne later. She only has two classes, both in the morning. She sits through them and doodles. She grabs lunch, visiting with her sorority sisters. She goes for a run and stops by the newspaper office to work on her next column. Some other paper people are there, and she gossips with them and does nothing else. To anyone else, it looks like she's doing the things she always does, but she's really somewhere else — in her head — the whole day.

Caitlin goes back and forth, debating. Shifting between being on and off the hook. Should she have been more curious to find out who the guy was that Anne liked when she first wrote? It didn't occur to her. Anne was so far away. What if Caitlin had known from the beginning that it was Peter — would she have told Anne then? *Oh, him.* Would she still have ended up with Peter, or would Caitlin have ruined their chances? How did Anne never meet him on campus? Because the girls were always together sophomore year and Caitlin avoided him? What if Caitlin had told Anne one of those many nights? *I had an abortion. Don't ever let it happen to you.*

When she gets back to the suite in the afternoon there's a note on the dry-erase board from Anne. *Meet me at Kelly's.*

Caitlin is still in her running clothes and grabs her Walkman and jogs the mile between campus and the bar. Anne is sitting in a corner booth and lifts her hand.

Caitlin slides in across from her. There's half a pitcher of beer in front of her and three jelly jars.

"Hey," Caitlin says.

"Hey, Buck," Anne says. "You just missed Peter." She fills two glasses and finishes off the beer.

"What did he say?"

"I didn't tell him," Anne says. "I'm not going to tell him."

Caitlin takes a long drink.

"Anne, why not?"

Anne rests her elbows on the table and cradles her face in her hands.

The waitress comes over to the table. "You girls okay? Another pitcher?"

"Coors Light, thanks," Anne says through her fingers.

Anne downs most of the beer in front of her.

"Oh, Caitlin, I can't tell him. He'd want to get married, right? Right?" She waits.

"Right." Caitlin takes another swallow.

"And you know I wouldn't. And I can't have a baby and give it up. Either way it would break his heart."

"Anne?"

"What?"

"What about your heart? What do you want?"

"I want to not be fucking pregnant." Her eyes fill.

Caitlin reaches across the table and holds Anne's hands in both of hers and they sit like that, bridging the scarred wood with their four arms. The waitress brings a new pitcher.

Anne lets go to drink again, then takes Caitlin's hand back.

"It's just bad timing is all. Five years from now, maybe this would be a whole different thing. That's what I first thought when we met. That the time just wasn't right. It wouldn't work out because we're just too fucking young. There's too much I want to do. I'm going back to Europe. Being married, having a kid. That doesn't work for me.

"Don't get me wrong. I love him, but I'm not going to be a

college bride like my mother was. She had to do everything *she* wanted to after she already had three kids."

"You're right about everything you just said, you know that, right? Anne, you do know that, don't you?" Caitlin says.

"Yes," says Anne. She's crying now, and Caitlin can see she's more than a little drunk. "I do. That's why I can't tell him. He loves me, and we can't go through an abortion together. So I'm not telling him."

"You guys have been together a long time," Caitlin says. Then, gently, "What happened?"

"Can we get more beer?" Anne looks at the table. "Oh, we have lots. Good."

She squeezes Caitlin's hands. "So you know the Pill makes me crazy, right? And he hates condoms. When it's safe, he comes; when it's not, he pulls out. Oh, God, I'm an idiot."

"Anne. Look at me. No, you're not."

"Boys always say, 'I'll do whatever you want, baby' in the bedroom, as long as it gets them laid. They never say, 'And if you ever get pregnant, I'll do whatever you want, no matter what it is, it's up to you. Accidents happen. You can always confess and be forgiven.'" Anne drains half her glass and refills it.

"I don't think they think that far ahead," says Caitlin. "I don't think they ever think it could happen. I don't know that it would matter if they did. They can say anything, but they're not the ones who have to go through it."

"Right," says Anne. "And I'm past the point of anyone saying anything different from what they said or didn't say. It's too late to revise anything."

"I know," says Caitlin.

The more Anne talks, the looser her talk is. It's all coming out. Caitlin won't let her order another pitcher.

"What did you ask me?" says Anne. "Did you ask me something?"

"I wondered what happened," says Caitlin. "You don't have to tell me."

"Right, no," says Anne. "I know." She puts her face in her hands again, then looks at Caitlin. "Remember that party Pax and those guys had? Did you go? Well, it was such a stupid thing. It was such a huge party, and Peter and I are making out in the hallway, we were going to leave and go to his place, then before I know it we're in some bedroom" — she drinks a long swallow — "and we're on the floor and he's on top of me and we're getting close and I said, 'Don't forget to pull out.'

"It was pretty loud, I guess, but then he comes inside of me.

"'What the hell?' I said. 'You didn't pull out?' And he said, 'I thought you said I could come.'

"'God, is there someone else in the room?' I said. 'I told you to pull out.'

"'I thought you said don't pull out,' he said.

"And then he goes on to say it will be okay, and I told him no, I really don't think it will. And it turns out I was right."

She talks and talks and Caitlin listens. When Anne finishes she lets go of Caitlin's hands and leans back against the dark wood. Her hair blends in with the walnut.

Despite what she might say, Caitlin considers, again, telling her. Right now. Altering the details — she could — so that Anne knows she can go through with an abortion. So she won't be so hard on herself; so Anne will know Caitlin's been there, too. To tell her at some point it will be well behind her, and she'll be okay.

"This wasn't supposed to happen. I'm scared."

"I know," Caitlin says. "Look at me. Listen. If you want me to, I'll go with you. I'll be with you there and with you afterward and it will be okay. We'll get through it. Trust me. And if you don't want to tell him, then don't tell him."

Anne slides forward, leans on the table, and laughs. "After all these years, all these boys, this has to happen now. God, even you and Peter had your little thing. At least he didn't get both of us pregnant."

She knows. And she doesn't know.

Frantic, thrust into this instant, Caitlin sees her choices, but which is the better one? Does she lie to Anne or not? Could she? She's managed till now, but this.

Caitlin breathes in and out, evenly and deeply, takes Anne's hands in hers again, and moves her head barely, from left to right. Sitting there, as the lights in the bar brighten while the sky outside dims, Caitlin will sacrifice one fragile reality for a more substantive truth. She's terrified, but leaps with faith to the place Anne has created that Caitlin has withheld and denied, but that has been there from the very start.

Masquerades

THE HALLOWEEN PARTY is an elaborate, upscale affair that Peter Herring's old college roommate Bobby Caruso and his family throw every year. Bobby, his parents, and his siblings all have their friends to their grand Short Hills home, less than an hour outside New York City. Peter and Anna decide to go as Dorothy and the Scarecrow after finding out another couple is going as Alice and the Mad Hatter, which was their first choice.

It was Peter's idea, an inspiration he had one morning a week before the party while they walked to the subway, shuffling through the fallen leaves and relishing the dappled sunlight peeking through those that hadn't. Some mornings there was frost on the car windows, and Anna savored the clarity of the brisk air in Brooklyn. Days like this were her favorite part of fall, and she knew they would soon be replaced by winter, a bleak time when she felt like she could never get warm.

"It's better this way," Peter said. "The Scarecrow—now, that guy had a steady head on his shoulders. And Dorothy—man, after what went down with the wicked witches, Alice is no match for her. This is a better idea all around."

Anna liked the change. In their short time together, Peter hadn't offered her anything that she didn't love completely.

Anna Riley graduated from college in the spring of '88. Weeks after moving to New York, she met Peter in a bookstore. That humid June day, Anna knew she had a fever and was getting sick. She was shopping for a book for her father's birthday. Peter was wearing a long trench coat and idled in the same aisle as Anna, who was trying to decide between a book about bridges and a mystery that had gotten stellar reviews. There was a homosexual element to the mystery that her father would dwell on and complain about, even if the book was a gift. But didn't her father already have a book about bridges?

Peter walked up to her and tapped on the bridge book. "You know, there's an even better one coming out this Christmas."

He was towering over her, standing too close in his unseasonable coat.

"Don't they make you check that coat or something?" she said.

"I work here, so they know I'm going to steal stuff," he said.

Anna stared up at him. Although she was sweating, she felt cold.

"I'm kidding," said Peter. "But I do work here."

"I'm getting sick," she said. "I'm freezing."

"You look kind of pale," Peter said.

"I've got to go. I'm dying," Anna said. "I'll get the mystery and tell my dad he can exchange it at Christmas for a bigger, better bridge book."

Peter walked her to the register and waited while she paid. "Thanks for your help," said Anna. She turned and made for the door. But just then a woman pushing a double stroller walked in, a bottleneck formed, and Anna was forced to step aside. She overheard Peter speaking to the guy at the cash register.

"I'm going to go out with that girl."

"Good for you. When's that?"

"I'm not sure. I just know I'm going to."

Three days later Anna went back to the store. She was finally feeling better and had decided to exchange the mystery for a less risky Civil War book. Her father seemed to accumulate books about the Civil War the way she bought black turtlenecks. Her closet was full of them.

Anna stopped at the register, then made her way toward the history section. She walked past Peter, who was shelving books. He stopped and followed her.

"Hey," he said. "May I help you? Are you feeling better? You look better."

"I almost didn't recognize you without your coat," she said.

"I'm working today," he said. "You know, you can buy more than one book at a time."

"I couldn't even think straight the other day," Anna said. "My dad would hate that book. I wish he wouldn't, but he would, so I'm getting something like all the books he already has, which I know he'll like because he keeps getting them."

Peter showed her the section she wanted and recommended a book that was a staff pick.

"Thanks," Anna said. "This is what I should've bought in the first place."

"Hey, I'm done at six tonight," he said. "Will you meet me after work? We can grab coffee or something."

"I'm Anna," she said. "Sure, I'll meet you."

Peter crossed his arms and smiled.

"That's good, Anna. Anna what?" he said.

"Riley," she said.

"Riley," he said. "I'm Peter. Herring."

"I know," said Anna. "I asked the guy at the register what your name was."

That night they met at the store and walked to a diner. They ordered coffee and grilled-cheese-and-tomato sandwiches. As soon as they found a booth, it started to drizzle outside.

"How's working at that store?" Anna asked him. "It's a nice one. So much good coffee. All that fine upholstery."

"It's okay," Peter said. "I'm on sabbatical right now, and it's a good fit."

"Sabbatical?" she said.

"Med school," he said.

"Huh," she said. "What year are you?"

Peter looked above her head as though he were crunching numbers. "When I left I think I was in my fourth week," he said. "All the men in my family are doctors — my dad and my brother. My other brother just started his internship. I guess it would be okay if I really wanted it. My family overestimates me. I'm trying to figure out if medicine is my thing. Maybe it is and maybe it isn't."

"'Sabbatical' doesn't really fit, does it? After only four weeks in," she said. "So it's med school or the bookstore for you?"

"The store's cool for now, but I'm not married to it. If I decide I want to go back to school I will, or I'll do something else. I don't need much to be happy. Besides, is there anything better than this right here?" Peter spread his arms, as if embracing the table, the remains of grilled cheese and coffee, and Anna.

Anna smiled. "What did your mom say?"

"She doesn't miss an opportunity to remind me that time is passing no matter what I'm doing," Peter said. "And I remind her not to worry, since I'm not worried. I've got no complaints. When I do go back, if I do, that's a different story. Maybe I will. I haven't made up my mind yet."

They talked about college and how they each came to the

city and who their friends were. Peter lived with two college buddies, Bobby and Michael, both of whom worked on Wall Street. Anna was an assistant publicist for the publisher of the Betty Crocker series of cookbooks. She'd found her roommate through a service.

"When I go on sabbatical, I'm going to travel, get a dog, or go to graduate school. Maybe all three," Anna said.

"No two are alike," said Peter.

The drizzle had turned into a downpour, and when it still hadn't let up after two hours, they left anyway and walked through the deluge to the subway.

"I want to see you again," Peter said.

"Can I kiss you?" said Anna.

"Well, yeah."

She leaned into him, and he rested his forearms on her shoulders and ran his hands through her long blond hair, tangled and darkened from the rain. There was nothing soft about the kiss, and as Anna pulled away from him, her top lip lingered behind, pressed between Peter's. Both of them were soaked.

"I have to go," she said. "I'll call you at the store."

She turned and ran down the stairs for the uptown train. Peter walked across the street, and by the time he got to the platform for the Brooklyn train, across the tracks, Anna was already gone.

Before Peter, Anna had slept with nine other boys. The first one and two others had been boyfriends, but the rest were only irresistible attractions, which once acted upon didn't last. She had liked the sex well enough and had climaxed when the boys who had worked to get her there relied on their eager mouths and clumsy fingers. But Peter was the first one she climaxed with from intercourse alone, and a week after they met, after the first time he found the spot inside her that no other boy had—which they nicknamed Herring's Harbor—Anna could count on four or five romps a day on the days they spent together, savoring her giddiness and spent muscles till their next round of what Peter called, simply, the good stuff. It felt to her like something they alone had created: their intensity for each other driving them to the point of exhaustion, followed by clammy sleep, food, and showering, reading, and talking, only to start the same sequence all over again a few hours later. She went on the Pill.

Anna stayed over at Peter's place because his roommates weren't home much and it was closer to her work than her own apartment was. On weekends they sometimes spent a whole day in bed, once even on a Monday, when they both called in sick after Anna had gone to Washington for the weekend to visit college friends. By Sunday, she was so consumed with missing him that she regretted the trip.

Peter taught her how to play chess, and when Anna won three nights in a row, he gave her a black T-shirt that said PRODIGY. It was her favorite thing to sleep in. One night before a performance of James Joyce's short stories, they made out in an alley, the gritty wall unyielding against

Anna's back. Peter lifted her skirt and all but slipped inside her. During the entire performance, she was distracted by her damp agitation.

In August, Peter took the king and queen of hearts from a deck of playing cards and stuck them to his refrigerator door with magnets, and directly below the cards he put up a photograph of the two of them taken at the beach earlier that summer. He showed Anna how the cards' profiles were oriented in the same direction, making it impossible for him to arrange them to face each other. He placed them so the king always looked toward the queen. Some days, when she took something from the fridge, Anna changed the cards around, and he always changed them back. When he had first put the whole arrangement up, it took Anna's breath away a little — she thought the display was so dear and telling — and every time she went to the fridge and looked at it, the cards reminded her of that first breathless happiness.

After three months, in September, Peter told Anna he wanted to look for his own place in Brooklyn and asked if she would move in with him. Without any hesitation she said yes, and they found a second-floor apartment in a brownstone in Bay Ridge.

Their costumes turned out well, and Anna is having a good time at the party. The guests have outdone themselves, and none have spared expense or time on their elaborate getups. Superheroes, Playboy Bunnies, farm animals, and aliens mix and mingle. Anna has been talking to Bobby's girlfriend, Jess—Peter Pan tonight—for the past half hour, but Jess is called away to help with some food. Anna takes her glass of wine to the backyard and lights a cigarette. A former classmate of Peter's, whom she met in a group earlier in the evening, walks out of the house toward her. He is dressed as a medieval monk.

"Mind if I join you?" He pulls out a pack.

"Not at all. But I'm sorry—will you tell me your name again?" she says.

"You're Anne, right?"

"Ann*a*."

He nods. "Paxton. Pax," he says. "Long live the class of eighty-seven!" He points the tip of his cigarette toward the house and raises his glass skyward. "I can't believe Caruso still has this fucking blowout every year. You still at that same flashy magazine?"

"Publisher, actually. Cookbooks. Betty Crocker," she says.

He frowns and sways perceptibly. "I thought you worked at that magazine where you'd interned before. There were over a hundred people who applied for the job you got or something." His confusion seems genuine, and Anna can see his mind working through it.

She holds his gaze. "You must be thinking of someone else. Excuse me." She leaves him and hurries inside to look for Peter or one of their friends. The house is loud and crowded with strangers and hazy in rooms where people are smoking. The sense of contentment she felt before talking to Paxton has vanished.

She asks people if they have seen Peter, but no one is sure, and she goes from one room to another looking for him. He isn't outside or on the ground floor, so she climbs the massive staircase to check the second floor, thinking maybe he hasn't wanted to wait for the bathroom. It is quieter upstairs, but the laughter and squeals float up from below. Anna hears a glass shatter and a woman's shrill voice bleat, "Oh, Kevin Keenan! My God, you're funny!" She checks one empty hallway and starts back down the stairs. Then she hears Peter's voice from a landing above her and stops.

"It's terrific," he says. "Books as far as the eye can see and any international newspaper I want at my fingertips."

Anna hears the other person laugh and is surprised it's a woman whose voice she doesn't recognize.

"Not exactly Columbia, is it?" the woman says.

"That was a different plan. You ended it. And my plans changed," says Peter.

"Peter, you always knew I planned to go if I got the job."

"Like I said, plans change. People can change their minds, make decisions all by themselves. You did. I did."

Anna hears the woman sigh. "So who's your new girl? Tell me."

Peter doesn't say anything at first, and it sounds like he is swallowing a drink. "It's a good thing," he says. "A good and simple thing."

"Anna. Right?" the woman says.

"Yes. Her name is Anna," says Peter. It's disorienting

hearing Peter talk about her, and her legs are feeling hollow and watery the longer she stands there.

"Well, what's she like? Is she dragging you back to med school?"

Peter laughs; that much sounds familiar to her. "She's not like that. She's also not moving to Europe or anything like that. She's not going anywhere."

The woman makes a sound. An exhale that implies a wealth of things unsaid.

"I told you at the very beginning," the woman says. "When we first met I told you that's what I was going to do. Maybe you weren't listening or didn't want to. Thought you could change my mind. Or didn't think I was serious."

Anna suddenly feels ridiculous in her blue-and-white dress and blond braids, and a feeling of panic begins to spread its way through her. She is still holding the glass of wine she'd been drinking outside. She downs what's left of it and makes her way up to the landing, remaining uncertain but hopeful with each step that her unsteady legs will get her there. Peter and the woman are in chairs facing each other. A bottle of red wine and two glasses sit on the table between them. Peter's scarecrow hat is on the floor.

Anna stares at Peter. "I've been looking for you." Her face is hot.

Peter's lips are a flat, compact line. He flashes her a grimace and starts to say something.

Before he can, Anna turns toward the woman and extends her hand. "I'm Anna," she says.

The woman unfolds from her sitting position. Standing on one leg, the other tucked on the chair's seat, she takes Anna's hand. Her grasp is firm, and she meets Anna's eyes evenly. She is dressed as Princess Leia, and it looks like her own dark hair has been swirled deftly into Leia's trademark buns. When she stands, the woman is shorter than Anna expected.

"Anne," the woman says. "I'm a friend of Peter's."

"I know Peter's friends," Anna says.

"Anne's an old friend," Peter says.

"I live in Italy," says Anne.

When Anne sits back down, Anna feels like an accident, onstage and unprepared.

"Just back to trick-or-treat?" Anna says. She can't look at Peter, but she can feel him watching her.

"Not exactly." Anne looks at Anna. Then she looks at Peter. "I didn't tell you yet." She gazes down at her hands clasped in her lap. "My mom's cancer is back. The magazine found me a desk in New York for a while."

"I'm sorry to hear that," Anna says. "I'll let you finish catching up." She races down the stairs, frantic to get back to the city. How has this surprise snuck up underneath her and shifted everything? She feels her eyes prickling, sharp and full. She scans the party and concentrates — searching for someone she knows, someone to get her back home — to keep from crying.

People downstairs are having a great time, the partying well established. She doesn't know anyone she passes.

"Kevin, knock that shit the fuck off!" somebody says nearby.

Peter finds her outside, smoking.

"Anna," he says. She waits. "Will you please talk to me?" His expression searches hers for an explanation.

"After you," she says.

"Look, I didn't even know she was in the country. I didn't know she would be at this party. I had no idea."

"Yeah, well, surprise," Anna says. "I didn't even know she existed. I win."

"Shit," Peter says. "Look, this isn't a problem. It doesn't have anything to do with us, with now. I went out with her in school. We were together, and then we weren't. She moved away. She moved to Italy, for Christ's sake."

"But she came back," Anna says. "A heads-up from you would have been nice, really, as recently as tonight. I had no idea where the hell you were. And then I found you. Both of you."

"I'm sorry," said Peter. "You were talking to people. Anna, there's nothing to worry about."

"For who? There's nothing for who to worry about?" she says. "I want to go home. I don't care if you come or not."

"I'll go, too," he says. "Let's find a ride back."

For the next week, Anna and Peter do everything as before, but with a splinter of unease between them. She wants to tell him what she overheard them say and ask him questions until he answers every one. But eavesdropping seems petty and childish now that it's over. When they talk, Peter says what he first said, that Anne is an old girlfriend and the relationship hadn't seemed important to mention, but now that things have happened the way they have, he is sorry that he didn't. He is sorry. He is genuinely sorry.

The weekend after the party is the New York City marathon. That morning they go out for breakfast, buy a paper, and divide the sections between them. Peter reads the editorials, and Anna does the crossword. Afterward they get coffee and sit on the curb among the crowds to watch the runners pass through Brooklyn.

"Man, that's not something I'm suddenly going to wake up one morning and have the urge to do," Peter says.

"It is quite a commitment," Anna says. "People find out what they're really made of."

"It's a race," says Peter. "It's not the marines."

When they get back to the apartment Anna takes a nap. Hours later she wakes up in the dark room groggy and confused. Peter lies sleeping on the bed, facing her. She undresses and presses her body against him and reaches down to his zipper. After minutes of her hand around him he opens his eyes.

Peter rolls her on top of him and presses his mouth into the shallow cleft between her breasts. "You, Riley, are my other half in the world," he breathes.

It's the first time since the party, and Anna is worried that their perfection in bed won't be the same, and it isn't—but it's the very opposite of what she feared. Their chemistry hasn't diminished, it's blossomed. After she comes, she sobs against Peter's chest, her tears as beyond her control as her climax. Peter runs his hands down her back until she quiets, and she thinks, *If only we could stay like this forever, everything would be okay.*

Afterward, Anna puts on the PRODIGY shirt and jeans. She goes to the kitchen and opens a bottle of wine and pours two glasses. She sits with her feet tucked under her while Peter cooks.

"You know, I was with someone my last six months of college," Anna says. She takes a large sip. "He was a cheater and a liar who fucked my roommate in my bed. At least he did the time I walked in on them. Until then he seemed like something completely different. The initial blow of bad news is always the worst part. That sick feeling where you can't eat for days and can only lie in bed sobbing. Finding you with Anne reminded me of that." She takes a second, bigger sip.

Peter turns from the stove and walks to the table. He sits down across from her. "Okay," he says. "You know I'm sorry, I really am."

Anna looks at him and waits, takes another sip. "You're not the only one," she says. "The only one with someone else before. But if I ran into him at a party, I would tell you. I wouldn't be able to not tell you. That's all.

"Before I walked up, I overheard you and Anne talking. It sounded like something really serious. How come she knew about me, but I didn't know about her? God, that asshole Paxton thought I was her."

"McNally." Peter shakes his head. "That guy has always been a dick."

"Why aren't you really in med school, Peter? Because she left?" Anna leans on the table toward him. "What was that about? What you said to her about me made me feel less than."

"Less than what?" says Peter.

"Than who I am," she says. "Than her, like a lower standard. You sounded bitter talking to her, like you're settling and you wanted her to know."

Peter sighs. "Her thinking I should go to med school gave it more credibility, more than just my family pushing it, you know, and that changed."

"Why did it change?" Anna says.

Peter runs his hands through his hair, leans back, and crosses his arms. "Okay. We're doing our life histories now, I get it. So here it is." He drinks deeply from his own glass. "I started med school, and she went to Italy with this magazine. I wanted some guarantee from her of us staying together, so last fall I went over there to propose. I surprised her. Not only did she say no, but she told me she'd been pregnant. Been pregnant. So she surprised me back. She didn't lie, exactly, she just withheld and delayed telling me something I should have known when it happened. It was over like that. And I realized I didn't really want to be a doctor, anyway."

Anna's eyes well up. She's crying more today than she has in months.

"It wasn't something I really wanted to talk about," Peter says. "That was the first time I've seen her. I'm sure someone at the party told her about us, about you. There were a lot of people there. It's not a secret."

"When you saw her, did you wish you were still together?" Tears stream down Anna's face. "Did you want her back? The truth."

"No, I didn't. Really," Peter says. "Look, I crossed that bridge and burned it behind me way before you and I met. Listen, whatever you want me to do, just tell me and I'll do it. I am sorry. If I could change everything, I would."

"Don't keep anything like that from me again," she says. "No secrets." Anna wipes her face.

Peter gets up, leans over her chair, and kisses her. "Done," he says.

On Saturday morning, the weekend before Thanksgiving, Anna folds the laundry they did around the corner right before Peter left to meet his brother Matt at the train station. When the phone rings she thinks it's him calling to say he forgot something.

"Hi," she says.

"Hello, Anna? Is Peter home? It's Anne."

"Oh, no," Anna says. "No, he's not."

"I'm sorry to call," Anne says. "I'm sorry if it's awkward."

"It's not for me," Anna says.

"It's just that when I saw Peter last week I told him my mother was wondering if he could come by and visit over the holidays, and he said he'd try. She's having a rough time, and so I thought I'd call and see when a good time for him would be. So I can let her know."

"When last week?" Anna feels like she is standing at the end of a long, dark tunnel.

"I stopped in at the store one day, and we had lunch."

"Oh, that's right," says Anna. "I forgot."

There is silence. "Can you please let him know that I called?" Anne asks.

"I'm very sorry your mother is sick," says Anna. "I really am. I can't imagine. And I don't even know you. So I feel very bad asking, but what exactly are you doing?"

"Peter and my mom were good friends. They played chess sometimes." Anne's voice starts to break. "I guess it sounds strange. I don't know. Everything is strange right now. I'm really sorry, Anna. I wouldn't be calling him. I wouldn't be bothering him if this wasn't happening. She really loved him. I'm not trying to cause any trouble. I told her I'd do this. Will you please tell him I called? I need to go. Bye."

Anna hangs up the phone and puts on her coat, scarf, and gloves and leaves the apartment. She walks up the street toward the bay. It's not even noon yet, but the sky is gray and darkening—an advancing bruise bringing a premature dusk. The wind is an assault she defies simply by remaining upright and walking against it. The intermittent gale blows in gusts and brings cold air down to the streets.

As Anna's face starts to numb, it matches the inside of

her. She recognizes the pit in her stomach. She replays Anne's words in her head until they don't surprise her anymore. The truth is always there; you just don't always discover it the way you would prefer to. She could leave. Won't it be better to have some control over how things go instead of waiting for the other shoe to fall? She thinks, *Leaving is so easy. It's staying that's hard.*

When she returns to the apartment, Peter and Matt are eating slices of pizza from the box open on top of the stove.

"Where were you?" Peter says. He leaves the kitchen and kisses her on the mouth and unwinds the scarf from her neck. "You didn't leave a note or anything. Your lips are cold. Matt's here."

"Hey, Anna," Matt says. "You want a slice? We just got it."

"Hi, Matt," she says. "No, thanks, not right now."

She takes off her coat and crosses the room and hangs it on the coat tree by the bay window. Peter follows her. "I went for a walk," she says. "Anne called here earlier."

"She did?" he says.

"You didn't tell me you saw her. She mentioned your lunch."

Peter puts his hands in his back pockets and looks at the floor. "Shit. I'm not ready for this," he says. "I've never done this before."

"Done what, exactly?" Anna says. God, she is tired.

"She came to the store one day," he says. "I've been trying to figure out how it would be if I went and saw Joan, her mom. Joan and I were good friends. If I decided to go, I was going to talk to you about the whole thing. I didn't know what to do. I didn't want to screw things up again. That's the only time I've seen Anne. She was pretty upset, so I took her to lunch. She said Joan thinks this is her last Christmas. I'm sorry I didn't tell you. I know you're mad."

"Do you want to go?" Anna asks. "Do you want to go see Joan?"

"I don't know. I've never known anyone sick like this," he says. "It would be the right thing to do, I think. Wouldn't it? Just a good and simple thing?"

Anna is still cold from the walk and clutches herself in her own embrace. She gazes out the window at the overcast sky, then down at the empty street.

"Then you should," she says. "If that's what you want to do, you should go and see her." Every passing second she cares more and then less and then more again about what she is in the middle of. She can't keep up with it.

"We both can," he says. He takes his hands out of his back pockets. He taps his palms against his thighs and steps toward her. "If you'll go with me. I'll go, but only if you come, too. Will you?"

Anna stares up at him. Would answers always be this hard to come by from now on? She thinks, *I'm not ready for this, either. Leaving is easy.*

"Yes," she says. "I will." The sound of her own words terrifies her, but they feel, equally, like the only ones she can say. "I'll go with you."

Legacies

As unfathomable as it is for Peter to grasp, on this bitter, brilliant Tuesday a week before Christmas, he and his girlfriend, Anna, are riding the R train from Bay Ridge into Manhattan to visit Joan Cavanaugh, his ex-girlfriend Anne's dying mother.

Because he has never known anyone who is dying and because Joan's imminent mortality seems so unlikely, Peter can't fully conceive of it and won't concede that she is dying. He is convinced that she and Anne are both frightened and, as a result, overreacting as a precaution. His own parents and his grandparents are still alive — in their fifties and seventies, respectively — and to Peter Joan seems like a more formidable foe for death than they do. If he were death, he thinks, he would pass by Joan and keep looking, wanting a sure thing. Someone who will go down easy.

Before Halloween, as far as he knew, Anne was still

abroad, so it was a shock for him to run into her at the Carusos' annual party, where he still saw many of his old college friends. The last time he'd seen her was in Europe a year ago, when he proposed and she dumped him. When she told him she had been pregnant. It was a two-for-one heartbreak. He underwent an intense mourning, longing for her, one that threatened to never end.

After the party he had done what he could to repair the awkwardness that had arisen between him and Anna because of Anne's unexpected appearance. Then, after things finally settled down with Anna, Anne called and told him Joan wanted to see him and asked if he would please visit. Hoping peace would prevail, he asked Anna if she would go with him, and without hesitation she said she would. So the awkwardness had not passed completely, not for him, but he took some comfort in knowing he had only himself to blame. He could have said no to Anne, but he could not imagine Anne telling Joan that he had refused to come.

When Anne and Peter had lunch after Halloween, she explained why she was staying on in New York.

Her doctor said it could be six months, she told him. *I said, "My mother didn't tell me that; why are you telling me that?" And he said, "Because you live in Italy."*

It was like he slapped me. Goddamn it, Peter. Goddamn it.

Peter had met Anne's parents for the first time at Christmas three years earlier, in 1985, when he and Anne were home for their semester break during their junior year in Italy. They went to her parents' first and then to see his family. Joan seemed so well then — and feisty, besides — but her disease had already begun its unrelenting assault.

Joan was not so unlike Peter's own mother, although Joan was a few years younger. But the most striking difference between the two women was that rather than presume to know everything about him, as his own mother did — he was the youngest of her three sons — Joan presumed to know absolutely nothing about him, as if Anne hadn't shared anything about her new guy. Instead, Joan set about asking, gracefully prying, and genuinely wanting to know what he thought about the program abroad and how he liked school and even what his politics were.

The mother of three girls — Anne was her middle daughter — Joan called Peter her vicarious son the second night of that Christmas visit. They had sat down to play chess. Joan was an avid player, but rarely got her husband or the girls to join her.

"You wouldn't mind, would you?" Joan asked him. He was feeling thoroughly in the spotlight, being evaluated, and so was on his best behavior, but he was unable to shake the feeling that he was like a fox in the henhouse.

"Mind what?" Peter said. He recognized that he was desperately losing the game and wondered how sick it was to have a cutthroat attitude toward the mother of the girl you were sleeping with and thought you might love.

"Being my vicarious son," she said. "These girls, who love, who truly worship their dad so much, they always remind me how much I need an ally of my own. Someone on my side."

"Aren't the girls your allies?" he asked. "You're all women."

She leaned on her elbows across the table toward him. "That is a misconception," she said. "I was one of five girls myself, so I always wanted boys, always. The five of us were never allies, not really, until we were all married adults — and even some days we're still not. You never know who's going to wake up that morning and turn the tables, shift the game on the rest of us, as women will. I love the girls fiercely, more than every other thing there is, but I think we'll be good friends, Peter."

After they had gotten to his parents', in Pittsburgh, Anne told him her mother was doing chemo and what he had thought was her hair wasn't really her own. Peter was first shocked, then pissed, that she hadn't told him Joan was fighting cancer — that she had lied to him. He said he felt like an ass being there during the visit and not being aware of something he should have been mindful of. If it were his mother, he said, he would have told her. But when Anne argued that she didn't lie, only selfishly withheld because she wanted to have a normal Christmas, introducing her new boyfriend and celebrating with him and her family, he acquiesced. He told her he was glad they'd been able to do exactly that. And also how sorry he was now that he knew.

After her diagnosis, there was Joan's mastectomy and chemo and radiation and treatments to annihilate spots on her lung and liver and a metastasis on her anklebone, but Joan prevailed, maintaining her unwavering humor and warrior attitude. Anne had regarded her mother's cancer — her mother's stage 4 cancer; *There is no stage 5,* Joan said — as Joan did, with all the concern of finding a ruinous permanent stain on precious fabric. Family and friends had followed Joan's optimistic lead, and the collective expectation was for remission and survival, of course.

So Peter had shaved his head in solidarity, against Anne's wishes — she loved his hair — but she had taken the razor and shaving cream when he insisted, after he'd buzzed it down as far as he could with clippers, and finished the job until his head shone. He stayed bald for months, until he got Joan's postcard: *Grow hair! I am! Love, J.*

After he came back from Italy, Peter and Joan habitually made time to have lunch or breakfast or a drink and visit, just the two of them. Anne always joked that she got the latest news about her mother from Peter because Joan told him more than she told Anne. Sometimes he felt flattered, and other times he would bluntly say to Anne, "Well, did you ask her? All I did was ask and listen. She'd tell you the same things if you'd been the one to ask."

Whenever he and Anne went to the Cavanaughs' for a visit, Graham, Anne's father, would announce their arrival, shouting into the apartment, "Joan, Peter's here!" Joan would appear from wherever she had been, and while she was hugging Anne — first, always first — she would be holding one of Peter's hands in hers, and as she ended the embrace with her daughter she would rely on her hand clasping his to transition to hugging him.

Now, on this December day, his visit to Joan imminent, he sits, passive, on the train next to Anna, who is wearing a new turtleneck and makeup to venture back into his damaged history, into this situation he feels outmatched by.

"Hey, Riley, thanks for coming," he says and picks up her hand. Her blue eyes squint, and she smiles at him through the sun. "You know we don't have to do this. I can just call."

Anna continues squinting at him, and he thinks she will pull her hand away, but she doesn't. "Yes. We do," she says. "It's important. I can always leave if you want me to and you can stay. Her mom is sick, Peter. It's good you're going."

"I don't really know what I'm doing," he says.

"I know," she says and smiles and shakes her head. She leans her weight on him and kisses him on the mouth, and he thinks he could stay on this sunny train car with her next to him, just like this, for a long time without wanting anything else.

They ride the R until they have to change for the 6. They emerge from the subway, walk three long blocks, and they've arrived. The doorman is attentive and holding the door for them.

"Good morning, Ian, we're here to see the Cavanaughs," Peter says and shakes the man's hand.

"Of course, Mr. Herring, so good to see you again," Ian, the doorman, says.

Peter says, "This is Anna Riley."

"Miss Riley, it's my pleasure," Ian says and extends his hand to her.

151

As they ride to the ninth floor, Anna's fingers touch his.

"Hey," she says. "I don't know these people, and they don't know me. You let me know what you want me to do, what you think, okay?"

Peter nods and puts his arm around her and the elevator doors open. Ian has buzzed the apartment, so Anne is there to meet them.

"Hi, guys, hey, Anna, thanks for coming," Anne says. She clutches their hands and steps aside to let them in. "Mom, Peter's here!" she calls into the apartment. *Thank you,* she mouths to him, and he nods and mouths back, *You bet.*

When Joan strolls into the foyer he is relieved. He had expected her to look worse from the latest radiation and the steroids. But her eyes are bright and her smile is coy, the way it is when she is telling a joke, enjoying wine, dancing, or beating him at chess. She has a silk scarf wrapped around her head, a rich swirl of red, gray, and orange.

She holds her hands up to her face and pats her own cheeks lovingly. "I'm so puffy," she says. "The moon is smaller than this face. Isn't it awful?"

"I can't even tell," says Peter.

"Take off your coats and come in, come in." Joan walks over to Anna, embraces her, and steps back.

"Anna, my dear, I can't thank you enough for sharing your beau with me for a few hours."

"Of course," Anna says. "We're happy to be here. Merry Christmas."

She reaches into her bag and takes out a wrapped gift

and hands it to Joan. "I liked these and thought you might, too."

Peter has no idea what the present is or when Anna bought it. Her gift is clearly only from her, not the two of them, and not having brought anything himself, he feels nakedly empty-handed.

"What a wonderful surprise. Let's sit and visit, shall we?" Joan says, taking the gift.

Then Peter leans over Joan and they hug as they always did, except that there's no Anne between them doing the handoff. Instead, in her one hand Joan holds Anna's gift, and as Peter embraces her under these new circumstances he feels a quiet panic.

Anne takes their coats, Peter and Anna follow Joan, Anne joins them, and the four of them sit. Anne opens a bottle of wine, and Joan opens Anna's gift — a set of eight coasters with lacquered reprints of famous paintings on the other side of the cork.

"Anna, my word, these are wonderful! Too nice to use, really. I'll have to hang them up," Joan says, turning and admiring each one. "Darling, just darling. Thank you."

"You're welcome. I'm so glad you like them," Anna says. "I got some for my mom, too."

Anne pours everyone a glass and sets out cheese and crackers and nuts and they all settle and sip.

"Peter, how is your family?" Joan asks.

"They're good," he says. "My parents say hello and send their love."

"I'll have to drop them a note," Joan says. "I didn't do my usual Christmas cards this year. Peter, your sweater is beautiful, and I just love the color on you. Dusky. Perfect for a day like today."

He glances down at his sweater and pulls it away from his body with his left hand and stares at it. "Thanks," he says. "Yeah, it sure is."

Anne is quiet, and when he looks up at her she looks down and tucks a dark twist of hair behind her ear. His sweater is more significant to Anne than Anna and Joan know. Anna looks at him, producing the telltale crease in her brow when she is curious, and then turns back to Joan, says how lovely the apartment is, and the visit is off and running.

Anne's younger sister, Carolyn, is there too. She appears without formality and hugs Peter and introduces herself to Anna. She hovers in the kitchen, taking care of dishes, slicing cheese, ready to tend to the four of them who are visiting.

Peter excuses himself. Already he needs a break and literal distance from the three women. He feels estranged in what was once his second home. The apartment is vast — Graham and Joan have been here for twenty-five years — and the walk through it is a kind of homecoming for him, a peculiar homecoming following a painful exile.

How many times did he brush his teeth here, load and unload the dishwasher, pour himself a beer, make love to Anne in her room after everyone else had fallen asleep —

the two of them covering each other's mouths so no one would hear their sounds? He knows every creaky floorboard and squeaky door hinge, and yet his familiarity with all these details challenges the fact that he is here with another woman, not Anne, not anymore. Although he has answered the phone here, prepared dinner, done laundry, and changed lightbulbs, he has to remind himself today, during this visit, not to act overly familiar, not to presume to help himself to that which is now off-limits and no longer his. Instead he focuses on being a gracious, modest guest, exempt from his former privileges here, and the vigilant work of detachment makes him self-conscious. He can't throw his coat on the bed in the room he stayed in so many times; he handed it to Anne, who will return it when he and Anna leave. He can't open the fridge or cabinets with authority, as he once did. He thinks of the expression "You can't go home again" and realizes the acute sadness those simple words carry.

He stops in the kitchen to talk to Carolyn. During his time with Anne, he knew Carolyn better than he knew Ceci, Anne's older sister — Carolyn was like the younger sister he never had, and he always thought she was more like Joan than her sisters were. Despite being the baby of the family, she always spoke her mind. She had a flirtatious streak.

"How are you, Carolyn?" he says. "It's been a long time. It's great to see you."

"I'm okay, considering," she says. She never stops moving while she talks. When there's not a dish or food to deal with, she wipes the counter. "I took this semester off from school. I've been here for everything. My dad needed help, and school can wait. She's going to be okay."

"I think so, too," says Peter. "This is awkward for me today. I'm glad you're here."

She hugs him a second time. "Man up, my friend. This is about Joan, not you, not Anne. I like your girlfriend."

"Yeah," he says. "Me, too."

"Go, get out of here," says Carolyn. "Don't be a pussy. Get back to what you're supposed to be doing."

He is in the bathroom for only a few minutes, thinking. On his way out, he glances in the mirror. *Fuck, why did I wear this sweater today? What idiot would do such a thing?* It was a crushing day on which he bought the sweater—the day he gave Anne the ring and she told him no. The fucking sweater. He can't even take it off. Underneath, he's wearing a black turtleneck with an unfortunate archipelago of bleach islands on one sleeve. And really, it doesn't matter. Not compared to Joan thinking this is her last Christmas.

When he returns to the living room, he feels more, not less, alienated from the three women. Joan and Anna are laughing about how badly Peter hates to lose at chess but pretends he doesn't. And Anne is smiling, too, complicit, because she was there many a late evening saying good night to him and heading off to bed while Peter and Joan played on. They are like three old friends, and he is the new kid, nervous about joining their game.

After he sits down, Joan says, "It is so, so good to see you again, Peter."

"It's good to see you again, too," he says and takes a long swallow of wine. "I'm so sorry things have gone this way. I'm not sure what to say."

"I'm not afraid to die. I'm not. I'm just not ready to go," Joan says. "And I don't want to get strange, since it's spread to the brain now, you know, I really don't. That's the only thing that worries me."

"Oh, Mom," says Anne.

In response, as if rehearsed, they are all reverently silent. Then, as their quiet is almost beginning to feel too long, Anna breaks them out of it.

"Do you have any pictures of Peter? You might not, but I'd like to see them if you do."

Anne and Joan look at each other. Joan says, "I have some in an album, I think. Can you find it, Anne?"

"Sure," she says. "I think I have one here, too."

Anne leaves and returns with a large, leather-bound photo album and a smaller one with a dark green cover.

Although this is awkward for Peter, Anna seems unfazed. They have been together for six months, living together for three, but have yet to meet each other's families or go to their homes. If they had already made those trips, Anna would have seen pictures of him that his own family has instead of a collection that an ex-girlfriend and her mother possess, evidence of a different version of himself.

Anna and Anne sit on the couch with the larger album

across their laps, and Joan stands up. "Let's play, shall we?" she says.

"Let's." He refills both their glasses and follows her. They sit across from each other at the table by the window, already set up with the chessboard. Joan moves first.

"She's really something, you know," she says. "To just come here with you today to get a closer look at who knows what kind of old girlfriend and her dying mother. That girl has a lot of pluck."

"You have no idea," Peter says and moves his pawn.

"Are you committed to her?" Joan says.

"Sure," he says. "We're together. It's good. We're having fun."

"Would you be chasing her to win her back if she left for greener pastures?"

"She's not," Peter says.

"So you think," she says. "Or think you know. But if she surprised you and did, would you? You have done that type of thing before."

Peter scowls and looks up from the board. "This is what you always do, Joan. I've finally figured you out. You start chatting me up, and I lose my focus." He continues his banter with her. "That's how you win. Distraction tactics. I don't know what took me so long."

"Then let's stop and visit first and then we'll play," Joan says. "You know, if I'm on my way out, I'm not leaving anything left unsaid to anyone, including you. We've known each other too long. I would be remiss."

"Okay," Peter says. "For whatever it's worth, I don't believe you're on your way out, and I didn't know there was anything left unsaid between us."

"I never got to tell you how sorry I was about you and Anne. I missed you, and I would have liked to stay in touch."

"I'm here now, and I'm not going anywhere, so we'll absolutely stay in touch. See how well all this is going?"

They still have not resumed the game, and Joan lifts the drapery and gazes out the window onto the city and then back at him.

"Everyone is on their best behavior at times like this," Joan says. "And they damn well better be.

"I remember when you and Anne met. She told me you'd had a thirty-hour first date. I knew then that whoever you were, you had to be something, because Anne, that one, she's single-minded and so driven like her father and picky about who she has along for the ride—because it's her ride, always, that you're joining. I remember thinking, 'I'm sure this boy is one in a million, but I don't think she'll have him—we'll have him—more than a few months.'"

"That's what happened, give or take a year." He laughs. "It's okay. It's not how she's built. I know that. Don't worry about me."

"I know about the pregnancy," Joan says. "How devastating that must have been. For both of you."

Peter is stung by her words. He is not frequently or easily caught off guard, but Joan has managed this spectacularly.

No response he can think of is a good one. Across the room, Anne and Anna laugh in unison.

"Jesus," he mutters. He would like to disappear.

"This is what I mean. About not leaving anything left unsaid." Joan sighs. "I never should have known. I went with her to her annual appointment last year when she came for a visit. We were going shopping and having lunch afterward. She filled out the form, and I turned it in when she left to use the bathroom. I don't know why I looked at it. I shouldn't have. I never should have seen it. I thought, she's my daughter, I know everything there is to know. I didn't, of course, and don't. No one ever does know everything about someone else.

"She was devastated and ashamed, and so was I. I felt like an awful snoop and a terrible mother. We both cried. She was sorry, and I was sorry, too. Sorry I couldn't help her at the time. Sorry that it was something she kept from me. She's my baby." Joan's expression is wistful. "We still had lunch. Not the lunch we were planning, but we still went."

Joan has opened a door that Peter has no choice but to enter. How he'll do that, under her scrutiny, he's not sure. This is not the visit he was expecting. Anna and Anne together have become the least of his worries. Joan's blunt foray into his past trumps his anxiety of what might happen between the two younger women.

"She didn't tell me, either," Peter says.

"She knew you wouldn't have wanted her to do it," Joan says.

"Right," he says. "Do you know what happened? Did she tell you? I flew to Italy, this great surprise. I fly over there and buy this sweater" — again he pulls it away from himself and agitates it a little; now it's a grim, convenient prop — "and a shirt for her at a real Benetton, right there on the Piazza di Spagna. I put the ring in its box in the shirt box. I wanted to marry her anyway. I bought the ring at Henne's. It was a big deal. And she said no. When she opened the big box and saw the ring box, without even opening it, she started crying and said no and it was over."

He pauses and drinks. He has been unleashed, like a faulty dam, not bothering to temper his anger for Joan's benefit, and thinks he should check himself. He traces the base of the wineglass with his finger and takes a breath.

"She said she had been pregnant at the end of our senior year and that she loved me and didn't want to hurt me but she didn't want this. She was so sorry that it was all happening after I had come so far. She thought me starting med school and her moving back to Italy would end things, but she said she should have known I would come and do this.

"Our last date was about thirty hours, too, in the same place. That's funny. I couldn't get over it, and I think that's why she told me. To end us for good. What's worse? She tells me about Caitlin, her roommate. Freshman year we had a little romance. I hadn't even met Anne yet. Caitlin got pregnant and never told me. Anne did. She was like a storm or a fire, something that leaves nothing behind. I left the day after I got there. Joan, I'm sorry. I'm sure this isn't what you wanted. I didn't plan on this."

"Of course I remember Caitlin. Such a dear friend of Anne's," Joan says. "They were just kids themselves, Peter. You all still are. You're closer to twenty than thirty. My word. What would you have done had you known? Married Caitlin as a sophomore? I don't think so. Given her money? Asked her to go steady? You hadn't, anyway — am I right?"

"They knew what they were doing. As much as a woman, a smart woman, is attracted to a man, or loves him, even, a smart woman would never want to capture a man under those conditions. Not for that reason alone. It never works out for anyone."

They are both silent, and her words settle over him.

"If I were you I might alter how I do my business in the bedroom." Joan offers this spontaneous, sunny suggestion, remarkably without judgment, although judge she certainly could.

And then, as Peter's treading his old and refreshed shame, Joan says, "You know, I was unfaithful to Graham not long after we were married. We got married right after college, and I had Ceci nine months later. I have ordered the girls, practically demanded that they do anything except get married at twenty-one. Do everything before you start a family. At least they are listening to me."

And while Peter is genuinely glad that Joan's daughters have made her proud with their compliances, he wants to fault a dying woman with her daughter's aborting his child and dumping him. Of course, at best, Joan is only indirectly responsible because of her own experience. And because in her opinion, not her daughter's, staying with him was not a desirable choice to make. Children defy and disagree with their parents all the time. Anne could have, and she didn't.

"Graham never knew," Joan says, "and it was only for six months after Cecilia was about a year old. He was my age, but he seemed both younger and older and so full of promise and mystery. He made me feel that way, too. And, my word, he was handsome! He wasn't married, and he couldn't believe I was. His grandmother lived in this building, and he would come to visit her and then me. We had our time while Ceci napped, and while I felt awful about it, I really did, he also made me love Graham more. Maybe to compensate, maybe because I felt like a catch again — who knows? Having this other man adore me and make me feel like a girl again — I still was a girl — but a married one, with a baby, and so uncertain of myself as that person. He helped — it's terrible to say, I know — but he did, he helped my marriage.

"I thought it might make a difference for you to know. Make you not be so hard on Anne. Please try not to be. Try to forgive her, even a little. None of us is perfect, and we all have secrets. We do the best we can, and sometimes our best is really only shit. Until the next day. Tomorrow is always another day to do the best we can."

"Jesus," he says. "What happened after six months?"

"He ended it. He said he was falling in love with me and couldn't continue the arrangement. I was never going to leave Graham, and he knew that. I was heartbroken, but I had no leverage. Within a year his grandmother died, and I never saw him again."

"His family didn't keep the apartment? In this building?" Peter says.

"Oh, his parents were from Westchester, always a little spooked by the city, I think. Not him, though," Joan says. "The apartment took quite good care of them, I'm sure."

"What was his name?" Peter says.

Joan looks at the backs of her hands, and her expression becomes distant. "I always called him Hutch. His last name was Hutchinson. And he always called me Joanie, which was such a hoot because I've never been Joanie a day in my life. Well, I was on the days I spent with him."

"You should get in touch with him," Peter says.

"Because I'm dying?" Joan sits back, and her gaze brazenly confronts him. "Everyone who needs to know knows. Everyone who is important."

"Well, he was, wasn't he? Important?" Peter leans back in his chair, too, challenging her. "If it was me, I'd want to know."

"Your generation is different," she says. "I think he's long forgotten, and no good would come from disturbing him and his family now."

"I get it," he says. "I'm just saying you haven't forgotten."

"Women are built differently. I don't think men cling and treasure the same way, have the same kind of memory. Or even care to."

"It depends on the person, I think," he says. "Fair enough. I appreciate your story and I'll try, I will, with Anne. I'm not bitter, not like I was. But it was us. I never thought she would have done something like that. Not to me."

"She was doing the best she could. Did you ever imagine yourself in her position? Men can never know what women go through. You can try, but you can't ever know."

She sighs. "I'm ready to play now if you are. I've had enough of the skeletons for one day, haven't you?"

"Yeah, I have," he says. "It's your move, Joanie." Although he is now the newly appointed, involuntary guardian of Joan's scandal, he feels like their personal scores are still far from even.

Joan laughs and boldly moves her rook. "And you're still working at the bookstore? When do you think you'll be finished with that phase? You may have decided medical school isn't right for you, but I should think you'd be awfully bored by now." He had always thought of med school as his and Anne's plan, and after he was only one, it didn't fit. Now it didn't fit with Anna, either.

"Getting there," Peter says. "Not entirely, but it's under way." That he met Anna in the store alone has made his stint there worthwhile. She was the first good thing to happen after Anne, and her almost identical name suggested redemption and do-over.

"I would imagine," Joan says.

"There's a lot about working there that works for me. At least for now."

"If you say so. Just looks a bit like slumming to me. Like turning your face to the wall, but maybe I'm overestimating you. Just be happy, Peter, do no harm, and don't waste time if you can help it."

By now he decides all he will do is listen until Joan says all she needs to, and he lets her have the last word.

Joan and Peter play while Anne and Anna scour both albums. Anne removes some photographs from hers and gives them to Anna, who tucks them between the pages of the book she brought with her for the train, then nestles the book into a secure corner of her bag. More wine is opened and more food put on plates. Graham arrives home and joins them, meeting Anna and coaching Peter as he slowly loses the game to Joan. Hours later Joan is tired, they all are, and it's naturally time for the visit to end.

As Peter collects their coats, he feels the weight of being watched and scans the room. His eyes meet and lock with Joan's. She is sitting on the arm of Graham's chair, absently stroking the back of his neck. She gazes at Peter with a complex combination of appreciation and another, elusive quality—raw and immodest. Caught, Peter flashes her a smile back and abruptly looks away. What a strange day. Although the pervasive disorientation of the afternoon is far from comfortable, by now he has grown used to it. Joan seems like someone he has just met for the first time, and the Anna leaving with him is a different woman from the one he arrived with hours ago. He feels the fatigue of having aged, as though he has undergone a crash course in the business of growing older.

In January, Anna and Peter invite Anne for dinner, and she brings a date, Sam, a St. Lawrence grad, whom she met at her gym. Anna and Anne not only seem to have developed their own relationship, but Peter observes Anne's deference to Anna, which surprises him — or, rather, Anna has moments of authority that she exercises over Anne, which he finds unexpected. It's a small thing: they are all discussing a movie, and Anne, who is mistaken, claims a certain actor appeared in the film. And Anna, confident, rightfully, of Anne's error — without being a bitch — gives her no leeway.

It's disorienting for him to cultivate a careful friendship with this woman — a woman with whom he was once so intimate. He has slept with many women and has never retained any ties to them once the relationships ended. This is uncharted territory with Anne. His new level of modest engagement with her reminds him that now he is just like most of the rest of the people she will interact with — the thousands of people who will never slowly run a melting ice cube up the inside of her open thighs, something Peter once teased her with on a hot August night while he whispered, *The iceman cometh.* The memory burdens him like a grudge he wants to shake but can't.

When he is around Anne, Peter consciously attempts to grant Joan the favor she asked of him, meting out forgiveness in Anne's direction in small, manageable portions.

Seeing if he can and how it feels. And sometimes, fleetingly and magically, almost, she makes it effortless for him. Without warning he will catch her eye, and something about the angle, the cast of her glance, will strike him as truly and gravely contrite. He doesn't long for her anymore, not as he once did. Anna is his recipient now. In lieu of longing, he now appreciates these expressions of Anne's, which he interprets as those of irreparable regret. When he catches them, they satisfy him in a way he never would have expected. He is dumbly grateful for them, and, in turn, he finds himself stretching his forgiveness farther.

Peter takes Joan to lunch once in early February. Later that month, he and Anna run into Joan, Graham, Anne, and Carolyn at brunch in Tribeca and join them. While nothing about Joan's cancer is off-limits, no one reports anything new, and it doesn't come up in discussion.

Peter tells Anna that although he isn't going to stay at the bookstore forever, he isn't going back to med school; instead he's registered for the LSAT. "It will break my old man's heart, but if he needs a good attorney one day, maybe I can help him out."

In early March, New York is hit with a freak snowstorm, and Anne calls him the same week: Joan blacked out that morning and came to on the floor. The previously known six lesions in her brain have become thirty. A week later Anna calls him at the bookstore after just hearing from Anne. Joan is in a coma, in hospice at the apartment, and everyone is just waiting.

Peter calls Anne to offer their help. She cries through the phone, says Ceci is home now, too, and there are so many people and so much food, and thanks but no, not now.

"All her friends are here. They sit around her bed and talk to her. My God, she's unconscious and all these women sit around and visit her like she's not. They were laughing about a hole in one and when someone lost a heel at the Barrymore one night. One of them was talking about her new grandson. I saw them this morning. I went into my old room, closed the door, lay down on the floor, and sobbed. I don't know what I'm going to do, Peter." Her voice is jagged, and she is teetering, inconsolable. "Remember when this started? I know it's stupid, but I never thought she was going to die. How can this get any harder? How can her being dead be worse than this?"

"It's all part of it, I think," he says. "What's happening now is all part of it. I wish it wasn't, Anne." He feels impotent and foolish saying this to her, and in a phone call, no less, but she thanks him. He wants to put his arms around her. It has been a very long time since he's wanted to do such a thing.

Anna tells him they should shop, make sure they both have something to wear.

Then on the night of March 23, when the phone rings, Anna is the one to answer it.

"Oh, hi. Oh. Oh, no. Oh, no. Oh, I'm so sorry. Oh, God. I know. I know. I know. Yes, yes, we will. Okay, hang on," Anna says. "Peter, it's Anne." And the wait is over.

He takes the phone. "Anne?"

She is congested and quiet. "She's gone. An hour ago. She died an hour ago." She sounds measured and worn, Peter thinks, fighting hard to hold back something whose will she is at the mercy of.

"What can I do? Can I call anyone? Do you have to call everyone?"

"We're taking turns," she says. "Dividing up the address book. It will be in the paper Saturday, and the funeral is Tuesday. Will you come?"

"We'll be there. Let me know if there's anything you need. Anything your dad needs. I'm so sorry, Anne." He manages to push all this out past the thickness filling his throat.

On Tuesday Anna and Peter take the train into Manhattan. The pockets of people at the funeral mass at Saint Jean Baptiste are dense and multigenerational. All Joan's sisters and their children are there. Caitlin is there, close to Anne. Friends surround Cecilia, but Carolyn is by Graham's side the whole time, her arm either around his waist or linked through one of his. She is the gatekeeper for her father, and while she is not remotely happy, she is serene and diplomatic, speaking for both of them when people approach, allowing Graham the chance if he wants to say more after she's finished with the greetings and thanks. When Peter and Anna go through the line, Caitlin shakes Anna's hand and hugs Peter. Anne hugs them both fiercely, Anna first.

A week later, the temperature has risen steeply, delivering a balmy April. Peter is home studying when the mail comes, and he walks downstairs to get it. There's only junk and a large envelope addressed to him in Anne's unique handwriting, all lowercase. Inside is a smaller sealed envelope with his name printed on it and a note from Anne. *i found this when we were cleaning out my mom's things. sorry no idea. i'm heading back to italy in two weeks, maybe see you and anna before? i'll call. —a*

He opens the second envelope and pulls out a single sheet of paper. On it is Joan's handwriting, in black ink, the script not quite perfect.

28 February 1989

Dear Peter, I think I'm getting funny. This seems silly but I've thought about our visit so I found him. Hutch. He has an office in the Trade Center. The girls and Graham are going to be going through enough so there's nothing I can do. But if you could, would you? If not, then never mind it. I'm glad I told you and thank you for giving Anne the forgiving. Hello to Anna and get on with it after the books. Don't wait. He's at Morgan Stanley, Hutch is. If you do it, you ask for Peter Hutchinson.

Much love— J

Handfuls

ON A FROSTY Saturday in mid-December, Palmer suggests they take a morning drive, and while Carolyn doesn't so much agree, she doesn't refuse. It's been five months since their twin girls died, arriving at a tender twenty-four weeks, unexpected as party guests who get the time wrong and intrude on hosts still sautéing, madly vacuuming. The time has alternately raced and dragged, and the need to don coats, hats, and gloves—heavy seasonal accessories that accentuate the grief they've been carrying—has snuck up on them. Carolyn and Palmer bypassed Thanksgiving, waiting out the holiday and Black Friday at home with take-out Chinese food, football, and rented movies. Thanksgiving night she went to bed before eight o'clock.

Even now, sometimes his wife eats and sometimes she doesn't. Faint points of Portland winter sunlight seep through their kitchen window while she drinks coffee and waits without complaint for Palmer to scramble eggs for himself before they head out. Once they are untethered from land, over the water and crossing the Broadway Bridge, his words break the silence inside the car.

"I think we're going in different directions."

Because he can't have this conversation in their home, their Volvo is the only ready arena to invite her into. A restaurant is no good. They don't go out anymore, and he needs to be doing something with his hands. Driving is enough of a task, but not too much. He steers with his right hand and twirls his wedding ring with his thumb, his left hand otherwise inert in his lap. He would never say such a thing if they were on the Fremont Bridge, which he knows Carolyn hates and is always anxious driving across because it's so high. He wants to be considerate despite the fact that he feels betrayed and is done. He wants out and away from the misery that binds them.

"No, we're not. We're both heading west." She scans the flat, murky Willamette River. "This should be their first Christmas," she says, her words as hollow as they are naked. The most naked she's been to him in months.

The car's heater is oppressive, and the luxury leather beneath him swelters his ass and thighs. Her words test his resolve, but only by the slightest measure. He feels the fissure in his chest, too close and heavy. He scrolls the driver's-seat thermostat to zero on the dash and cracks his window so that the bracing air can give him some relief.

"I know," says Palmer and steels himself. "I meant it figuratively. We've moved away from each other."

*　　*　　*

On a stifling July day at the end of her second trimester, Palmer and Carolyn had taken refuge in a movie theater for a matinee when her contractions started—for no predictable reason, the doctors said later—contractions that all the drugs couldn't stop. Then, when there was no turning back, although Carolyn had pushed and pushed, labored so hard, Palmer thought, the girls had slid out into the world as effortlessly as ice cubes thawing in the sun.

Grace, born first, hung on for a week after their birth, and her sister, Abigail, a mere fifty-two hours longer before the sparks of their lives fizzled out, their fledgling hearts and lungs lasting as long as they could, the available technology impotent. They never even opened their eyes. They were so small Palmer could hold each of them in the center of his open hand.

But before they had left the hospital, all four of them, Carolyn had cradled each daughter's body—swaddled for home but bound for the mortuary—against her own and rocked in the glider. She had been dry-eyed while she hummed "Itsy Bitsy Spider"—twice—but Palmer had not. When they switched places and he had rocked each of his lifeless daughters, she left the room, but he could hear her keening outside the door.

Days later, sitting in their bed at home, calm and coherent on Xanax, Carolyn had said, "You know, Palm, maybe that was their destiny. What if I couldn't handle it? I might have had something postpartum and smothered them or thrown them off a bridge while you were at work. This way, at least, I'm not locked up."

He'd had to take a walk alone and weep, again, until he was spent. Her crazy rationale — while medicated — shocked him. That she could think such a thing, let alone say it, was proof that she occupied a darkness of which she'd revealed just a glimpse; it was proof that he was in over his head much more than he knew. The only response he could muster was to leave the house.

Selecting the caskets had furnished the most torture. They were cartoonishly tiny, conjuring for Palmer shoe boxes in which people buried a dead bird or baby bunny found in the yard, yet such coffins were manufactured, so they couldn't be the only ones with a need. You shouldn't be able to pick up a coffin for a person with your own two hands. You needed to call on eight strong men, or at least six. That was true when his grandparents died. He wasn't sure he and Carolyn would make it through the task, but what had held them up had been the funeral director, Matt MacKay, and his gentle comfort and sympathy, devoid of pity, as he helped them choose. He was a pro, to say the least, and his compassion shifted — but didn't relieve — Palmer's anguish. During the morning they spent with him, MacKay had quietly shared the story of the loss of his and his wife's second child, a girl, to SIDS decades earlier. His mortuary had buried her. Now their four grown children were in their twenties and thirties, the two eldest working in the funeral business alongside their father.

During their appointment, Carolyn, without provocation, defended their choice for burial.

"I know they were barely here and so small they barely were, but I can't imagine burning them up," she said. "In our family when someone dies, we bury them. We go and visit."

When she was nineteen, Carolyn had lost her mother, Joan, to breast cancer. Palmer had never known Joan, only her legend, but he had visited her grave every time he and Carolyn had traveled to New York. She didn't even have her mother to nurture and console her. In Joan's absence, her three daughters mothered each other.

Nonetheless, Palmer was infuriated that she had uttered such a macabre thing about their daughters' bodies. Her insanity has no bottom, he thought, and she's taking us deeper and deeper. I'm just as off my nut, he condemned himself, that I'm going down with her.

But MacKay, unfazed, had put his arm around her shoulder while the tears rolled down her face.

"You're doing the hardest thing a parent ever has to, Carolyn. Those visits will be important, and when you make them you will remember how brave you were today."

Carolyn composed herself enough to say, through trembling lips, "We don't need two. Put them both in the same one. So they'll be together, like they were before. That's all they know."

"We'll do just that," MacKay assured her. "They won't be alone."

"I pushed them out," said Carolyn. "I should have held onto them longer, closer." Her body cast downward, and she spoke as though she were in the room alone. The two men just listened. There was nothing either of them could say. In the silence, Palmer felt his value as a husband diminish and his failure as a father expand with every ticking minute.

The flood of condolences had been both a blessing and a curse. It never stopped, and while the giving of food and flowers and cards had been, of course, what people do, Palmer felt a silent gratitude from the heart of each bene-factor clinging to every offering they received: *Losing a child — two at once — thank God it didn't happen to us.* There had even been a bouquet of Mylar flower balloons that Palmer methodically sliced open with a blade of his Leatherman, one by one, and put in the trash as soon as he found it on the porch. He didn't even read the card. He didn't want to know what asshole had thought sending such a thing was a good idea. After the trash had been picked up, he had some regret that he couldn't go to the sender and say, "You? You send a bunch of fucking balloons to the parents of two dead babies?"

His parents, younger brother, Fritz — not married, just a tomcat kid in his twenties — and older sister, Sybil, who was married with no kids, all lived in Portland. They ro-tated so at least one of them was there daily. Carolyn's fa-ther, Graham, flew out from New York as soon as the girls were born and stayed until he had given all the help he could. He transferred the food people brought from their dishes into Tupperware containers and marked the lids with the date. He loaded and unloaded the dishwasher and washed the Pyrex pans by hand. He sat on the couch with Carolyn tucked against him if she was awake. If she was asleep and there were no dishes to tend, he didn't quite pace, his heart obviously wasn't in it, but he systematically walked the rooms of the house with his hands folded behind his back, stopping at random to gaze out the windows. Beyond that the man didn't seem to know what to do any more than Palmer did. Carolyn's sisters, Ceci, who had three kids, and Anne, with a five-year-old, flew out, too — from Boston and Brooklyn respectively — managing the few visitors who were allowed while the cooler on the porch was discreetly filled, emptied, and filled again by friends. They were like a troop of Mr. Magoos, Palmer thought one night, sipping Scotch with Graham. *We're all but colliding into each other in this house as we march our own blind marches.*

He has tried to be the guy she married. Not pushing, not rushing, not pretending, talking when she wants to, holding her when she cries, withstanding her futile punches to his chest, her silences, her two solid days of uninterrupted sleep. He knew it was sleep only because he checked up on her regularly to make sure she was still breathing. They had not done fertility treatments, and neither of them had multiples in their families. They were both thirty-one. All they had done was have unprotected, cozy sex on a gray February afternoon. The girls weren't supposed to arrive until almost Halloween. Maybe, if there had been only one, the doctors said, she could have made it.

Their sitting vigil, desperate, for so many hours, had made no difference. The two separate phone calls had come from the hospital anyway, mere days apart, because twice they had left—the first time only drained, the second, bereft. They had heeded the neonatal nurse's advice— *Go home and get some rest*—because she was an expert, wasn't she? But leaving—first two babies, then one—had been the prelude for, in their absence, their older daughter dying, then their younger. The girls' hands were so little that Palmer had been able to slide his wedding ring over them, even when they were balled into fists. With room to spare.

It's all still raw for him, but he's had to return to work and make a living at the agency, which is not only Portland's premier ad house but also an internationally renowned group that can hold its own with the best creative minds in the world. Like the food people brought, working helps but also doesn't. Although he excels at his job—salvaging deals that are in jeopardy, drawing the hard line, negotiating circles around the most entrenched client—early on after he came back to work people avoided him and even his gaze as they passed him in the lofty corridors. The agency sent an enormous bouquet for the funeral mass, which was private, and an equally elaborate food basket to the house, but only two people said anything to him: his boss, Jim—who calls him Palmer "the Closer" Kurtz—and Jason, his tightest colleague there, whose wife, Robin, was pregnant at the time. Jason sobbed against him during his consoling embrace. Now Jason has baby pictures of his son on his desk.

One night Jim dropped off a fine bottle of single-malt Scotch, handing Palmer the gift after they shook hands.

"I hope I'm not out of line," Jim said. "But I thought you should have this on hand. Might need it." And Jim was right—he had.

They had met at his office. Carolyn had gotten utterly lost in the agency's labyrinthine building, where a few nonprofits leased space. She was headed to one to pick up a pamphlet about volunteering. Palmer was leaving to move his car to a fresh meter, and she asked him for directions. She was desperate, she said, and fretted that for ten hopeless minutes she had retraced the same unproductive steps. He got her to the organization she wanted, then saw her again when she was leaving and he was coming in.

"Thank you," she'd said. "Did I thank you? You need a beacon to navigate this joint."

"You're welcome. Again." He was glad for the second chance. Long, dark, careless hair; clear, expressive eyes he wanted a longer look into; a fickle dimple. A woman who looked like she did and volunteered. "I can get you out of here, too. How about having a drink with the beacon?" That was the start of them, five years ago.

Carolyn is a counselor with a master's degree, but she hasn't returned to work. "You're an emotional ambulance chaser," her sister Cecilia teased her when she started her practice. Ceci had sent her a *New Yorker* cartoon of two women, one telling the other, "We can't be friends if you won't let me fix you." Her other sister, Anne, had sent a wallet-size affirmation card with the calligraphed quote *We laugh to survive* and had written on the back: *Dearest C— Remember, it's true! You're going to need to laugh a lot!* Carolyn had tucked the card into a corner of the mirror over her dresser, but after the girls died it was gone, and Palmer had no idea where it was or whether Carolyn still had it. While it was true that his wife was ambitious, hungry to relieve the mental sufferings of others, and deft at doing so—preventing suicides, preserving marriages, directing addicts to rehab—the ability to heal herself was outside her realm. The support group and brief counseling they'd tried hadn't helped. She was untouchable the way physicians are dreadful patients—they know as much or more than their caregivers and are therefore immune to the restorative powers of hope that work on a layperson.

She is still smart and fiery, even pressed into the depths of loss. But what did it mean that one day while he was at work Carolyn repainted the girls' room, weeks after they died, covering the buttery yellow they'd done in May to a dull blue that reminded Palmer of a shiner? He supposed the project was proof of her ability to survive, but it wasn't the proof he wanted. She still wasn't small enough to fit into her regular clothes, so she wore Palmer's jeans, refusing anything maternity, and although she wasn't even good at cutting in, which Palmer always did, the paint job was flawless. But he wanted the feisty version of Carolyn—the one who would drink too much red wine with him, fuck him until they were both spent, get pregnant, and have a baby, healthy and full-term. Just one. The odds were in their favor. The doctors said so. But Carolyn had returned unopened boxes of merchandise without a receipt: two Graco car seats, two First Years bathtubs, two BabyBjörns.

"They wanted to give me store credit," Carolyn had told him after she took it all back. "And I said I wanted a refund. The manager gave me one when I told her why, but she wouldn't look at me."

Carolyn had challenged the doctors and their advice: "What if we're a bad match? What if the two of us only make babies who are doomed? You know, it's remarkable to wish for something you never thought you would wish for. I wish I'd had a miscarriage, that they'd died inside me. That I'd never felt them move."

"You think we're a bad match. Wonderful." Palmer had spoken louder than he intended to, and an unplanned laugh came out, too. "Losing the girls is enough, goddamn it. Can we confine the catastrophe, please?"

He knew the doctors hadn't known how to reply when confronted with Carolyn's raw candor and the couple's acute marital crumble. But she and Palmer were desperate for someone to bear witness, and maybe provide rescue. Rescue her. Us. *Please,* Palmer thought, *someone.* The comfort the doctors gave relied on rote clinician script. *We're so sorry. Many couples are stronger after a loss like this. You love each other and want a family, so you should try again. There's no reason not to.*

But last Saturday night, a week ago today, at an agency dinner, Carolyn had given him a searing reason not to. In spite of her routine rejections — when she pleaded she couldn't, he wasted no time taking care of himself in the shower, and once in the car on I-5 driving to Seattle for a meeting — she had drunk too much, even for her, and had kissed Anders Gregory, a potential client, seated next to her. Palmer had had to beg her to even attend. Gregory was in his sixties and sported a complexion indicative of a lifetime of drinking. In their three years of marriage, neither had ever strayed, or been tempted to, but there Carolyn was right under Palmer's nose, flirting with an executive his company was courting. Not exactly an enemy, not at first, but not a friend, either. Gregory caressed his goatee and gazed at Carolyn while he tended her wineglass, so it never emptied, and Palmer contained his outrage when Gregory followed her from the table. A few minutes later he went looking for Carolyn and found Gregory holding his dick at the urinal and met his wife staggering out of the ladies' room. When they returned to the table, Palmer ordered her black coffee and didn't let her out of his sight.

Sitting in their bed the next morning, with coffee again, he asked her what happened.

"Nothing. We talked about breast cancer. His wife died, too. I got to talk about my mom."

"Bullshit," he said. It wasn't enough for him, and so he pressed. "Did you kiss him?"

Carolyn's nod was a sucker punch to his gut. He thought nothing could top losing the girls, but her devastating admission was on par. In that instant he was a man whose house had burned to the ground, nothing recovered.

"That was all," she said. "Nothing more."

"Jesus Christ, Carolyn," said Palmer. "That's enough."

"He made me forget who I was for a little while."

"That's not a fucking reason. He made you forget me, too. You were loaded. And what guy does that with another man's wife, right in front of him?"

"I'm sorry." That was all she said. "I'm so, so sorry."

Since the party, briefly, he has reconsidered his agency's relationship with Anders Gregory's corporation and, seriously, his own with his wife.

Palmer drives across the bridge and down into the Pearl District.

"What the fuck are you trying to say, Palmer?" Carolyn says. "God, do I have to say for you the thing you can't say yourself but I know you're thinking? 'Carolyn, I want a divorce.' Tell me I've ruined everything. Say it."

This is the fire that he can't imagine being without, but he can't foresee their future, either, though the idea of leaving her is a different thing entirely now that she has uttered it—impossible to imagine. It was less awful when it was just an unspoken, vengeful whisper tugging at his mind. They seem to have moved not at all, unearthed nothing of their ruin, still frozen in the same place they were when the girls died, but now there's this new rubble to sift through.

"You don't know what I'm thinking," he says. "You have no idea."

If they split, who would have him? Or her? Dating would be a minefield. *Yes, I have two children I visit. No, you don't have to worry about being a stepparent.*

He has won over the toughest clients in the business without breaking a sweat—he's Palmer "the Closer" Kurtz, for Christ's sake. He can simulate walking away, but always saves the prize. He hasn't campaigned hard enough, called on all his talent to right things after their horrific setback. It's his fault they have gotten so far afield.

"I don't want a divorce," he says. "I don't want you to want one, either. And if you do, I'm going to fight with everything I have. I don't care what it takes."

Carolyn drops her chin and pushes out her words between sobs. "Can we go visit them? I'm so sorry, Palmer. Will you take me? Please don't leave me, please."

They are parallel with the waterfront, and he scans for a place to park. He can't drive with his cold, shaking hands, his hot mind, not right now. He needs a little time. Nothing more.

"Yes," whispers Palmer. "But I need a minute."

This is the first time she has asked to go since they lowered the tiny box next to his grandparents' graves. They have never seen the single black granite marker they ordered, adorned only with the girls' names in bronze, mounted in the order they were born:

GRACE

ABIGAIL

He finds a spot and manages the car to the curb, thanking God for learning to parallel park in a mammoth station wagon.

He turns off the ignition and reaches for her. She has showered this morning, and coconut wafts from her hair. Her scent summons their honeymoon, on Baja. He sees her cocooned in a cabana, lathered in sunscreen, reading, nursing a Negra Modelo with extra lime, dominating a black bikini. Slim, fearless, laughing, sprinting across the beach ahead of him. Her snorkel, mask, and flippers dangled and flapped from her hands as she left agitated sand in her wake. His only apprehension as they submerged had been losing sight of her in the Sea of Cortez, so he followed her fins or swam beside her as they explored the aquatic unknown. He was never in the lead. He remembers, too, back in their room, how he savored the mingle of sunscreen and sun-dried salt under her jawbone, along her clavicle, as he licked and kissed his way down.

He clutches her thin torso, shrouded in the bulk of her wool sweater and down coat. He cradles her head in his hands and rests it on his chest. He runs his fingers through her long, dark, clean curls. He buries his face and inhales the coconut again. Does their *after* outweigh all their *before?*

Better the devil you know, Palmer decides and trembles, weeping and clinging to her, incapable of letting go. *My devil.*

Kitten Season

5:54 a.m.

SHE GETS TO leave. After Lindsay clocks in, Margaret, the animal-care tech who has had the same overnight job at the humane society for fourteen years, buys a Pepsi out of the soda machine, as she does every morning, and goes home. Lindsay's team has been killing animals for the past two days, and they have another day of it ahead of them before they switch to the cattery for their three-day rotation there. Lindsay starts at six o'clock, cleaning the dog kennels—the "hallways." This is how she's started every Saturday morning for almost two years. She knows what she's doing.

She flips on the lights, which provokes a chorus of barking among the almost 150 dogs. The shelter has seventy kennels. Most contain two dogs each, and the puppy kennels can hold up to six. The dogs are conditioned, having been here long enough to know the drill, and they are poised and coiled, waiting to hurl themselves through the guillotine doors when Lindsay lifts and lowers them, locking the dogs out. She has to encourage some dogs toward the outside runs when they'd rather lean against their gates and smile and wag. As grim a place as this is, the friendships are as powerful as they are short.

Lindsay turns on the radio loud, and music competes with the din. She primes the steam cleaner and goes down the aisle, alternating sides, as the dogs head out to their cold, dark cement runs, where they'll leave more shit and pee. She gets to her favorite, Arlo, whom Lindsay keeps thinking she'll adopt if his time is up and he's still here, even though she already has two dogs of her own. Every time some cool young couple comes shopping in the hallways, Lindsay tries to sell them on Arlo. She talks to the dogs as she lifts the metal doors.

"Hi, Arlo; morning, buddy," she says, and out he goes. "Hi, funny girl," she says to a shar-pei, the ugliest dog breed there is. "You're new." Lindsay looks at her paperwork. The dog's name is Sunshine, and she is two years old. Reason for release: Can't keep.

The animals have come here for ludicrous reasons none of them can believe: moving to Minnesota; having a baby; chewed siding off the house; landlord won't allow. The animals are regrets, afterthoughts, even if they came first. Sunshine scoots out, and Lindsay taps the door closed behind her. There's not a ton of shit to scoop this morning, thank God, and no painters. Some dogs crap overnight and then, like preschoolers with finger paints, tamp and dance in their poop and not only smear it on the walls of their own kennels but also mash it into their gates and the chain-link fence that separates the kennels up to the ceiling. This will go fast today.

She passes the empty kennels of six dogs named Buddy, five named Max, four Sams, eight Bears, and pushes in the gates as she makes her way down the line. She gets to the end of the row, turns around, and doubles back to close the rest of the guillotines that she'd hooked open. She thinks all the dogs are outside now. The barking is ever-present background noise as kennel mates cavort and neighbors gnash teeth at each other through the chain link.

6:09 a.m.

There's one dog still inside, about halfway from the end. He is pressed up against the gate so his tufts of hair look like quilted mounds against the diamond-shaped pattern of the metal.

"Hey, kid," Lindsay says. "Who are you?" She looks at his paperwork. Teddy. "Time to go on out for a bit so I can clean."

She closes the guillotine door, flips the bracket on the

gate, and steps into the kennel. He's a medium-size dog, a shepherd mix, maybe, and not keen on going out this morning. She clutches the scruff of his neck to ease him toward the door and pulls on the cable with her other hand to lift the guillotine, but the dog doesn't budge. Lindsay gives his scruff a hard tug. "Come on, Teddy, out you go," she says. This happens sometimes, too, and right about now the dog usually realizes he's going no matter what and gives in. But not Teddy. He sits down, increasing his distance to the outside run. All right. She releases the cable, and the guillotine door closes with a dull metallic smack. Fucking dog.

"That's a boy, Teddy." Lindsay steps closer to him and gets a harder hold on his neck. Her fingernails bend backward. She raises her voice. "You're going out now." She doesn't have time for this. Pissed and wishing she had a leash or collar, Lindsay tries to yank the dog by his skin across the floor to the door that's now closed. She extends her right arm, looks up, grabs the cable again, and lifts the door. Teddy growls.

She hears it as much as she feels it through her hand. Teddy keeps sitting. The dog will not move, and as he stays, dug in, so does the growl. It doesn't stop. It's low, deep, and constant. For how long—ten seconds? Five? She doesn't know what to do. *Fuck. Fuck. Fuck.* Lindsay stands still. There's no one else in the shelter. The next shift starts at seven, almost an hour from now. She barely moves and takes her hand off Teddy's neck and—without seeming to, she hopes—shifts her feet away from the stance she'd just had, next to the dog's own feet. The growl continues as he stares at her and bares his teeth.

Despite her terror and tiny motions, Lindsay tries to seem invisible. She doesn't look at the dog, and now she doesn't move at all. Her eyes land everywhere but on him, and her heartbeat competes with Teddy's growl. How long will they stay like this? The only upside is that she still has the cable for the door in her right hand, and the open space to the outside run beckons. She'll just keep holding it. Maybe he'll go outside on his own. He finally does. Stops growling and staring, trots right past her and through the door. Lindsay closes it after him and exhales. She hadn't known she was holding her breath. Her legs are liquid, and her eyes fill. She feels as solid as tissue. She swallows and pulls Teddy's paperwork out of its plastic sleeve and puts it in the pocket of her scrubs. Reason for release: Not enough time for dog.

6:52 a.m.

The first person to arrive after her is Fritz Kurtz, whom Lindsay wishes was her boyfriend, she thinks, but she for sure wants to sleep with him. It almost happened one night a month ago after a bunch of them went out drinking. Fritz and Lindsay left the bar and walked to the house she shares with her three housemates. They were making out for a while, and things were going pretty well—his Carhartt jacket and Doc Martens were on her bedroom floor, and they'd gotten their hands down each other's pants—and then the rest of the techs showed up on her porch and started banging on the front door, so that was that. That night, while they were grinding against each other, Lindsay asked him, "Who names their kid Fritz? That's a dog's name."

"Germans," he said. His mouth crushed hers. "People who want their kid to save animals."

"Is that even your real name?" she said.

That was the most intimate conversation they've ever had. She could barely make eye contact or talk to him before that night, and she has struggled more since. He rides his bike to work. She's always loved a boy on a bike.

Now that Fritz is here, Lindsay stops cleaning to tell him what happened. He's a team leader, and his team is the one in the hallways today, trying to get dogs adopted. To go home.

"Hey, Fritz." He's on the other side of the break room, putting his stuff away. He shuts his locker door and waits. "This dog almost went after me this morning. You should check him out." She gives him the paperwork.

He takes it, scans the page, and looks at her. "He hasn't seemed like a problem," he says. When he talks to her she remembers how he smelled and tasted, and her neck gets hot.

"Well, an hour ago he wanted to kill me." She leaves to finish the kennels.

9:23 a.m.

The shelter doesn't open until eleven o'clock, but already most of her team is in the receiving wing, screening the dogs released the day before and getting crates of cats who are PTS: Put to Sleep. The team in the cattery is evaluating cats and bringing them the ones who aren't adoptable. It's April — kitten season — and the fact that there are a lot of people who think it's a good idea to let their cats get pregnant have made for a busy day ahead in kennel 9 — their nickname for the euthanasia room.

"Hey, you guys. Morning," Lindsay says to Barbara and Amy, who is her best friend here.

"Hey, Linds, how's your day?" Amy says.

"You know that dog Teddy? He was a complete dick this morning; refused to go outside. Scared the crap out of me."

"I can't picture him. Who put him out?" she says. She's vaccinating an Australian cattle dog. Blue merle. The dog is wagging its tail and panting.

"Michelle's team. I pulled his paperwork and gave it to Fritz. What's this dog's story?"

"'Not enough room.'" Amy laughs. "What is wrong with people?"

"All kinds of stuff," says Lindsay.

10:01 a.m.

In an hour people getting rid of their animals will bring them in, and people wanting pets will start shopping. The shelter has two different entrances — one for surrendering and one for adopting — and Lindsay's always wondered: What if people just traded pets in the parking lot

among themselves? Amy and Lindsay empty the freezer
in kennel 9 that contains the bodies of all the animals
they euthanized yesterday. They toss the cold, rigid, awkward shapes — huge and tiny brown plastic bags — into
the gray wheeled bin the size of a sports car that they
slalom through the shelter's property down to the crematorium at its lower edge. They run the crematorium
every morning so that by the next day the animals' ashes
are cool enough to shovel into buckets they toss in the
Dumpster, as though they were ordinary trash, before
loading the crematorium with a new batch of stiff bodies.
They set the dial to preheat, which will be followed by the
cremate cycle, and push the empty bin up the hill and
back to the building.

11:02 a.m.

They're open. Barbara and Stacy, the team leader, stay in
the receiving room taking animals from people while
Karen screens dogs for adoption. Amy and Lindsay stay in
kennel 9 and start euthanizing. At least they won't have
to deal with the public today, only their shitty decisions.
Michelle's team in the cattery keeps bringing them the
day's cats to kill. They are sneezing, feline-leukemia positive, or pronounced PTS because they're out of space and
they've been here the longest.

The real estate in the kitten room is precious and competitive, and it's pure Darwin in there: you look good, you

play good, you bump someone who doesn't. And with so many kittens to pick from, the adult cats' chances of getting adopted are diminished at best, desperate at worst. As the adults languish, passed over for the more darling choices, the more apathetic they become. You can almost see their countdowns start right before your eyes.

After people abandon their cats in receiving, the techs walk the carriers back to the cattery and leave them on the floor. As more cats come in, they stack the crates as many as five high. The rows and columns of carriers start to resemble walls a child might build with blocks. Except each box has whiskers and wide eyes—one face or even four or five—peeking out its front door. As the other team screens the cats and puts them out in the cattery's adoption kennels, the structures are disassembled and rebuilt in kennel 9. The cats that don't make the cut come back to receiving, and the walls are simply relocated, cat by cat.

They use sodium pentobarbital—SP, blue juice—which is kept locked and carefully logged, because it's a controlled substance and sometimes people filch it to get high. Amy and Lindsay alternate holding and injecting the cats as they deconstruct the walls of carriers, emptying one after another. They both have good IV skills, and it's easy for them to find a vein on the adult cats. But the kittens they have to do intraperitoneally, IP, into their abdominal cavities, because their veins are just too small. They do one cat after another and cover the bodies with a towel so the next one doesn't see them. Before long they have a stacked wall of cats' bodies on the table — fat males who smell like spray, kittens with gunky eyes, brown tabbies, tortoiseshells, and blue point Siamese — who for whatever reasons are here and dead in a pile instead of home somewhere basking in a sunny spot. Their names fill the lines in the logbook: Buster, Tommy, Midnight, Sweetie, Mabel, Zoë. They check that they're gone by a needle stick to their hearts, and when none of the syringes moves they slip each cat, one by one, into plastic bags, tie them closed, and lay them in the freezer.

12:03 p.m.

Lindsay goes to lunch and, because it's the weekend, the shelter is packed with people looking for a pet. The shelter's new slogan is *Got Pets?* — mimicking the milk campaign — and it covers billboards all over the metro area. Lindsay glances at the faces as she threads her way through the crowds. She wants to stop people at random and ask, *How long till you're back saying it didn't work out?* She passes Teddy's kennel and, although he's there, the plastic sleeve where his paperwork should be is still empty. She doesn't see Fritz, but the rest of his team is talking to the public as they show the dogs and explain their breeds and personalities and promote spaying and neutering, crate training, premium foods, and feeding on a schedule. There's a man who keeps interrupting the tech he's talking to. Lindsay can't hear what she's saying, but every time the tech starts speaking he repeats the same refrain: "Yeah, yeah, got it, right, no problem, you bet, absolutely."

A couple is standing by Arlo's kennel reading his paperwork and scratching his chin through the gate, so Lindsay stops to rewind the hose across the aisle and listen.

"This says he's a medium dog, but he looks pretty big to me," the woman says.

"He's smaller than a bunch down there on the other side," says the man.

"Should we get someone to take him out for us?" she says. "He's been here for four months. He's so cute. Who would give away a dog like this? It says on here 'Can't keep.' What does that mean? Is something wrong with him? What will happen if he's not adopted? Will they just put him down?"

Get the fuck away from him! Lindsay wants to scream.

"I thought you liked that female, Tawny or Candy or something."

"Ruby," the woman says. "I don't know. It's just so sad, I don't know what to do. I did like her, I do. Should we get her, do you think? Her thing said she's not good with kids, though, and we're having kids someday. Maybe we can train her to like kids before then."

Christ.

"We've gone without a dog this long," he says. "No one says we have to get a dog."

"I know, but I've never had one," she says. "I want to. I

think it would be fun. There are people with dogs every-where, and it looks so great."

Assholes. Lindsay finishes with the hose and keeps walk-ing.

After lunch she stretches out on one of the couches in the break room. There's still forty-five minutes before she has to clock back in. Believe it or not, once you've worked there long enough you get so used to the constant barking that it's possible to fall asleep twenty, thirty feet from the racket right outside the door. To power-nap as you would in any workplace at midday. It's not that you stop hearing the din, it just stops being something that keeps you awake. Lindsay's done it so many times that her body automati-cally wakes up in time for her to punch in on schedule. Over her sleep, she hears the beep of the microwave, murmurs of people coming and going, laughing and eating and rattling lockers, but when she opens her eyes the only other person in the room is Fritz. He's sitting at the table by the door with his arms crossed, watching her.

1:08 p.m.

When Lindsay gets back to receiving, Amy is fretting over a black kitten that Michelle wants PTS because she's con-vinced he has Manx syndrome.

"He does not have it," Amy says. "He was just wormed, so he has some diarrhea, and, yeah, he has a short tail, but he's fine. He's a great little guy. He's sneezing, so he should be fostered. Michelle's such a fucker. She never wants to foster anything."

"I'll take him," Lindsay tells her. The kitten is about ten weeks old and black with green eyes. While Lindsay holds him he bats at her earrings, and when she puts him on the stainless table he makes a syringe cap skate and chases it. Lindsay and her housemates have fostered cats before, and they've all gotten well and been adopted. A friend of theirs adopted one and took her home right from their house after paying and filling out all the forms. Amy runs it by Stacy first, and then tells Michelle Lindsay will foster the kitten.

The afternoon flies by as they get through all the cats and kittens and several feral cats that arrive in squeeze cages, trapped by concerned citizens who live in neighborhoods where feral cats are rampant. People wait while they transfer the cats to the shelter's cages so they can get theirs back. They euthanize the feral cats IP—just as they do the kittens. They are so wild the techs can't touch them, so they manipulate the cats' bodies into a corner of the traps to inject them where they need to, in their stomachs.

The receiving room is full of people, and the team's getting backed up, so Stacy pages for assistance. One man's bringing in a bitch and her litter of four puppies—the bitch is so aggressive that the postal carrier will no longer deliver mail to the man's house. They tell the guy she's not adoptable and that if he's going to leave her with them she will need an owner request for euthanasia. The puppies sound fine, and they say they'll screen them and try to get them adopted. The man's eyes are vacant as they explain the paperwork, and then he agrees to the owner request for the bitch.

"Shit. Just a goddamn dog," he says as he returns the signed forms. "Okay, you can have the pups, too. They're real nice." They follow the man to his truck to bring in the dogs. With his help they manage to get the bitch on a control stick and Stacy scoops up the pups. Just as she's contained their wriggly bodies the man says, "I think I'll keep this one. Take her back home with me." He plucks a puppy—the one female—from Stacy and leaves her holding the three boys. The man clutches the girl to him as Stacy walks away from the car with her brothers. Lindsay's disgust is tapped and floods through her. The puppy he's keeping is going to turn out just like her mother. Amy and Lindsay lead the bitch to kennel 9, as though she's a caught fish on the pole. They'll have to sedate her—with an intramuscular shot—before they can safely get close to her vein.

A couple and their two little boys bring in the body of their ten-year-old chocolate Lab, Gatsby, whom they want a private cremation done for. Gatsby had cancer, and their vet came to their house this morning to put him to sleep. His family wants his ashes back to spread in their yard. The boys are blond and little. Their father sits between them on the bench in the room, an arm wrapped around each of them, while the younger one sobs into his hands and the older one buries his face against his father's chest. The woman's face is red and puffy, and it takes her awhile to complete the form because she keeps stopping to blow her nose and blot her eyes. In one hand she clutches a wad of crushed tissues that peeks out between her fingers. Her husband stands up, and he and the boys — as though they're one person — walk to the counter. He rests his hand on the back of her neck and watches her write. Each time she stops writing, he leans close to her and says the same thing.

"Anna, do you want me to fill it out? I can fill it out. Let me fill it out." And each time she shakes her head hard, says, "No, Peter," and starts writing again.

Amy and Lindsay take the stretcher to their station wagon and carefully lift the dog's body onto it. "Can you please keep his blanket with him?" the woman asks in a wrecked voice.

"Sure," Lindsay says. "We'll call you when he's ready to come home. In about a week. I'm really sorry." They have a smaller crematorium for the privates, which is where Gatsby will go. None of the dogs people give away has a name like Gatsby.

"Thank you so much," she says in a raw whisper. "He was such a hero."

2:52 p.m.

There's a knock on the kennel 9 door, and Amy and Lindsay yell, "Come." Fritz opens the door and walks in with Teddy.

"Lindsay." He hands her the leash and gives Amy the paperwork. "He's PTS," he says.

Amy reads the paperwork. "This is the dog from this morning?"

Lindsay nods.

"I think he's gone a little nuts here," Fritz says. Lindsay looks at her shoes. Fritz leaves.

In this room she realizes how small the dog is. His ears are pinned back, and his tail is tucked. He yawns wide one time and licks his lips, then his mouth is tight. He squints.

Amy says, "You want to hold or inject?" Just like she has all day. The whole shift they've alternated as the animals have come in — they have to.

"Hold."

As good of a friend as Amy is to her — and she is; it's like they're married here — she hasn't gotten a chance to talk more about what happened with Teddy. They have been so busy. Lindsay was waiting for the right time, for more time. To tell Amy about how scared she was those long minutes while he stared and growled at her.

At the cabinet, Amy draws up the dose and records it. He weighs fifty-eight pounds; Lindsay weighs a little more than twice that. She was so afraid he was going to hurt her, but could he have?

"This dog is going to die because of me," Lindsay confesses.

Amy turns around and walks over with the capped syringe. "Because of you how?"

Lindsay stares at the blue liquid in the shot. "Because it was me the thing happened with," she says. "Maybe he wouldn't have done that with somebody else. He hasn't been here that long."

Before Amy responds Lindsay already knows what she's going to say.

"Lindsay, if it hadn't been you today maybe, maybe he would have gone home with someone, and what if it was someone's baby he turned on, some kid who pulled his tail? Then what? If he did it today he'd do it again, maybe, maybe not, but if he'd done that to me this morning, he'd be here just like he is right now. He would."

"I know," Lindsay says. "I know you're right."

"And Fritz signed off on him. He wouldn't have if he thought the dog was fine."

Right, she thinks.

But Lindsay wonders: What if Fritz had been cleaning? Would Teddy have done the same thing? If he had, would Fritz have given him a pass? What if her hand had been on the back of his neck five minutes later—would that have made the difference between compliance and that steely stare? Was she too rushed? She could have started cleaning and given him some time, and he might have gone out on his own.

Was it his fault or mine?

"You want to muzzle him?" Amy says.

"Yes."

The dog sits, and, anxiously, Lindsay puts the muzzle on Teddy. He's frozen in the same spot the whole time. She kneels on the concrete floor behind him so that he's between her legs. She wraps her left arm around his neck, under his throat, and braces her left hand against the back of her own neck. Her left forearm is the only thing between their faces. Amy waits while Lindsay picks up the dog's right front leg with her right hand and rolls the vein with her thumb until it pops up.

"Ready?" Amy says.

"Okay."

She hits the vein on the first try, pulls back, and gets blood.

"Release," she says. Lindsay does, and Amy injects.

The dog, like a balloon deflating, crumples as the drugs go in, and he's gone. They bag him and put him in the freezer with the others.

"See you tomorrow, Linds," Amy says. "Take it easy, okay? Call you later."

"Sure," she says. "See you tomorrow."

3:12 p.m.

Lindsay makes her way through the crowds to the break room and clocks out. She peels off her scrubs and takes her fleece jacket and backpack from her locker. On her way to the parking lot she stops in receiving to pick up the carrier with the black kitten, a litter box, and baggies of food. It's pouring rain. She runs the cat to the car first, puts the carrier on the floor of the front passenger seat, and goes back for the rest of it.

Her windshield is fogged over. This always happens when it rains. Her car is a beater with a crappy defroster, but she cranks it on anyway and, reluctantly, the haze recedes. Two small scallops of clear glass bloom at the bottom of the window and slyly climb up the outside edges. A wide, stubborn strip of condensation stays rooted down the middle.

Lindsay watches the parking lot and waits for the fog to clear. Empty-handed families with smiling, expectant faces stride through the adoption entrance. Two people carrying cat crates to the receiving door tilt with the weight of them. A frenzied dog straining at the end of its leash drags a resigned woman, wet and annoyed, so she almost collides with the cat people.

She closes her eyes. She wants to leave, but she still can't see well enough. She'll stop for a mocha on the way. When she gets home she'll take her dogs to the park. Fold some laundry.

She opens her eyes. Families file out of the adoption office cradling cardboard cat carriers with the shelter's name and logo printed in blue ink on the side. Two new owners emerge from the building, grinning—elated—as they are dragged through the lot in opposite directions by an amped-up dog and a gangly puppy pulling on cheap nylon leashes. The one with the dog passes a woman who's just left receiving—the dog lunges to sniff her—she's empty-handed except for the wad of leash she carries and its dangle of leather. Two men exit the receiving door, walking erect now that their empty carriers have been relieved of their previous weights.

Lindsay pushes away intrusive thoughts about Fritz and Teddy. Imagines Teddy wagging his tail and smiling at her and going outside when she encouraged him the first time. Pictures pushing Fritz onto his back in her bed — no drunken friends banging on the door to interfere with the clothes piling on the floor and their bodies warming closer and tighter until there is no space between them. Both things surge from the corners of her mind, but she won't think about them and makes them freeze at the edges. The window is finally clear, and she shifts into first. When she lets out the clutch the kitten mewls from the floor. Maybe she'll keep this one.

Collateral

To KEEP BUSY on Saturday morning while she waits for the movers bringing her dead parents' things, which she and Peter decided to keep and ship to the northwest, Anna Herring loads the dishwasher. Her father has been gone for a month after going it alone, such as he did, for three years without his wife, Penny. Now Anna is a middle-aged orphan.

Anna, Peter, and their boys flew to New Jersey, again. Anna's sister, Meg, and her family came down from Connecticut. Together, they buried John Riley and dismantled and divided his apartment. Anna and her sister have picked out two final sets of clothes, planned two funeral masses, selected two caskets, buried two parents, and emptied two closets, twice donating the decent things to Goodwill and Saint Vincent's and throwing in the Dumpster what was unfit to pass on — stained underpants, socks with holes, tattered bras, transparent boxer shorts. Just like that, after a week, the death business was taken care of for their second parent: Penny and John's apartment, no longer theirs, was empty and ready to rent, and everyone went back home.

"Well, that's the end of that," Meg said when she dropped Anna and her family off at the airport.

Anna thinks she should have something to show, besides merely surviving, for having withstood the two losses, dissolved her parents' existence, and come out the other side.

At the sink, she rinses and dries the previous days' pots and the Teflon and Pyrex pans. For months before her mother died, she prayed for God to take Gatsby, her beloved dog, and spare her mother, whom she couldn't imagine life without. Eight years of Anna's success as an equestrian first as a child and then as a teenager, had made her closer to Penny than Meg was. Closer than Anna's friends had been to their mothers. Years of lessons, early morning horse shows, tantrums when the pony didn't cooperate, recoveries from falls. It was what the two of them did together. Her father hadn't allowed them to have dogs or cats, and while horses and ponies weren't exactly pets, they were animals that Anna had deeply connected with.

When Anna started begging for the dog's death and her mother's survival, it was because both were battling cancer: back east, her mother, at sixty—metastatic breast-to-brain—and in the northwest, Anna's and Peter's eight-year-old chocolate Lab, a bone cancer survivor but every day vulnerable to the disease silently spreading to and ambushing his lungs.

The first time Anna made the negotiation she felt the usual guilt of betraying someone you love, but Gats had enjoyed more than his share of borrowed time. By the time Penny was terminal, the dog was two years past the amputation of his left hind leg—a situation in which twelve months was the most generous life expectancy. Gatsby broke the curve. Anna's attempt at deal making with God was in vain, of course, but at least she felt she had made the genuine sacrifice of Gatsby on her mother's behalf. Anna had done what she felt able to do, offering what she could for her mother, but it hadn't mattered.

One night she had begged on her knees and pledged that she would kill the dog herself if, in exchange, divine intervention would heal Penny. All she needed to proceed was a sign. She wished for a dream. She thought of the Old Testament sacrifices, in which only an apparition showing up in time prevented terrible tragedy. So much action based on faith. So little doubt. Faith in the face of doubt. Faith was not her strength, and she knew it, and she had wanted to order up a version of suffering she could endure and find some proof of God as a result. Gatsby ultimately outlived Anna's mother and died when his time came, sixteen months after Penny's. For that year, with her mother gone and the dog by her side, Anna was left with her paralyzing grief, her incessant crying jags after she dropped the boys at school. But she'd gone on because she had to. The boys

needed her, and Peter did, so she indulged in her break-
downs when she was alone and had ample time to drain
her sadness before she had to fulfill any other commitment.

Included in the whole uncharted insanity that came to
her after Penny died was her temptation to track down
Peter's ex-girlfriend, Anne. The two women had met when
they were all in their twenties, when Anne's mother, Joan,
was dying, her breast cancer taking the same lethal course
as Penny's had. Anne and Anna had been friends in the
briefest, most careful way and had liked each other despite
the circumstances, or because of them. Peter had loved
Anne more than she loved him back, and Anna loved Peter
because she couldn't help but do so. When she and Peter
had gone to Joan's funeral — it was distressing to grasp that
someone Anne's age could lose her mother — Anna felt
great sadness for Anne while she comforted herself with
the belief that her own mother would live well into her
nineties and ultimately surrender to her body's simply
wearing out.

But since her father's death, Anna has battled cloying
bouts of guilt. John's death — she began referring to him as
John in the weeks before he died — has caused her a much
more shallow grief than her mother's did. In the wake of
John's death, Anna has mostly been afflicted by her own
glaring mortality, now that she and Meg are technically
next in line to go, but that's the extent of it. She tries to re-
call memories of her father that are pleasant, devoid of fear
and shame.

He helped her buy her first car, a day she remembers fondly. It was Lent, and so her father wasn't drinking. He'd had patience and humor with the salesman, with her. She had the car for thirteen years. Then there were the animals: although he wouldn't allow his daughters any pets, he had had dogs growing up, and when Anna and Peter got Gatsby as a puppy, John told her the story about saving his dog from being electrocuted on the railroad tracks when he was a boy. She had no way of knowing if the story was true; there was no one to ask about it now. It was hard for her to imagine her father as a child, devoted enough to a dog to save his life in such a risky circumstance. But when she did drum up occasional flickers of her father's boyhood, she thought it was cruel of him to have had that love for a pet yet deprive his own children of the same.

Anna returns the dry pots to their cabinets and wipes the counter. She is tired and moving slowly. Anticipating today, she tamped her discomfort last night by drinking a bottle of wine by herself and watching the three latest episodes of *The Good Wife* on her laptop. Where *will* they put her parents' things? How bewildering to bring their furniture and pictures — half her mother's jewelry and photo albums — into a house neither of her parents ever saw.

A wave of numbness thunders over her. What is happening to her face? She can't feel her lips, frozen in a pucker. She's dropped the sponge. Her hands are palsied claws. Is she having a heart attack? A stroke? Some undiagnosed fatal condition that people never see coming? She's going to drop dead right now, in her kitchen, while she waits for her parents' relics?

"Peter," she can barely call out. Where is he? "Peter, where are you?" She sits on one of the kitchen stools. Her hands and lips clotting inward. Her face immobile. So much tightness. The boys are in the playroom next to the kitchen. She won't have to yell for them to hear her. "Jude? Brian?"

Brian, their ten-year-old, comes into the kitchen. "What's up, Mom?"

"Sweetie, will you find Dad? I'm not feeling well."

"Sure," says Brian and saunters down to the basement. "Hey, Dad!"

Seconds later Peter sprints up the stairs with Brian behind him. "Sorry, I had headphones on. I was lifting. What's up? Are you okay?"

"No. I'm having a stroke or something." Anna squeezes the words out through her clenched teeth. "I can't feel my face or my hands. Look at me." She glances down to direct his gaze to her gnarled fists. "I think I'm going to die." Her chest feels pinned by some invisible pile. "Will you please call nine-one-one? I'm afraid I'm going to die."

She notices Brian staring at her. "Sweetie, go back and play. I'm just not feeling well. It's okay. We'll get some help," she manages.

"Is Mom going to die?" Brian says. "I don't want you to die, Mom."

"I don't know what's going on, but Mom's not going to

die," Peter says, his lips against Anna's forehead. "I'm right here." He rubs her back.

"I'm about to pass out. I want you to call. Please call, Peter," she says through gritted teeth.

"Okay, I will, it's okay. I'm right here. Keep talking to me. Brian, go back in with Jude. Go back and play. I'll get the phone." He picks up the kitchen cordless, rests his other hand on the back of her neck, and dials.

The mornings he is awake at 4:30, Kevin Gallagher closes his eyes and prays for Jimmy Sullivan, his dead best friend, and for Jimmy's wife, Brenda. Kevin has to get through another day living and moving the weight of his person through the world without Jimmy doing the very same — a situation he's been in since 9/11. Kevin and Jimmy had been each other's best men and firefighters in the same house. They had been as close as brothers.

It's been nine years, and the amount of time Kevin still thinks about Jimmy varies on any given day. If he is up at 4:30, Jimmy may stay with him till noon as Kevin talks to him in his head.

Man, the baby's teething and she won't sleep. You should have seen the play Jeter made Tuesday night. Brenda is okay. I know you want to kill me. It didn't have anything to do with you or Alyssa. Don't judge me, brother. We both loved you, Sully. This is what he says to a dead man.

Kevin believes that on the mornings he is not awake early, even in sleep, the most reverent, purest part of his

So Much a Part of You

mind still pays a nod to Jimmy, misses him, and apologizes humbly. Says one more time, *I would trade you, buddy, it's worse here. It's worse here without you.*

Kevin and Alyssa don't even live in New York anymore, and that left Brenda behind with the rest of the ruin. Of the rumors about widows and surviving firefighters, Alyssa had said, "I don't get it. I could never do such a thing if you had died. Sneaking around with a friend of yours — of ours — for what?" she'd said. "How do they think that's helping? That they're fixing something that can't be fixed?"

He knew Alyssa felt lucky, grateful that Kevin had had a flat tire on 17 South that terrible morning, otherwise he would have been at his firehouse on time, with all the other men, some who had died and some who hadn't. Jimmy had spent the night at the station, his first of two on. Kevin was overlapping a night with him, starting his own two on. During the men's three off, their families were going camping together. Tents, camp stoves, and sleeping bags were staged in the living rooms, ready to load in the cars. The spirit of summer refused to wane. The month was still so lovely.

Kevin called Alyssa between Monroe and the city — in the middle of his seventy-five-minute drive — so she already knew, by the time the devastation had begun and the phone networks were clogged and she couldn't reach him, that he'd been delayed and hadn't made it to where he was supposed to be.

215

His call had woken her, and he remembers her groggy "Hello?"

"Babe, it's me," he said, "I have a goddamn flat."

She replied with a sleepy hum. Then "You okay?"

At that hour, the sky muddied as Tuesday's shy morning bled into Monday's retiring night, and the air on the side of the road was quiet and poised.

"Yeah, just pissed," he said. He held the phone between his chin and shoulder as he opened the trunk. "Sorry, darlin', but if I'm stranded in the dark on a highway, it's your voice I want to hear. Only for a minute. I'm going to be late as it is. Go back to sleep."

His firehouse was in the Bronx, but they had wanted it both ways. Alyssa needed her garden and yard, and they had their wonderful black Lab puppy, Emmett, to consider. Jimmy and Brenda were a few miles away, in Sugar Loaf. The shift schedule made both lives possible; that's what he and Alyssa had decided. Their daughter, Meghan, was a baby, and Alyssa didn't want to be by herself for days on end in someplace that wasn't her own. Their being in New York at all was a temporary compromise—Alyssa's accommodating Kevin in exchange for the permanent roots they were going to put down when they moved west, back to the coast she loved. That's the sole reason they were in New York in 2001 at all, because Kevin wanted one more year in the place he'd been born and called home before he left it for good.

*　　　*　　　*

"Hey, sweetie, the fire truck is here," Peter says. "Hang on."

Anna has clutched herself through the minutes since Peter dialed. "Fire truck? Where is there a fire? I'm having a heart attack," she says.

"I just called nine-one-one and said what was happening," he says. "They sent these guys, I guess."

Peter opens the door and shakes Kevin's hand. "Hi, I'm Peter," he says. "It's my wife, Anna. She's in the kitchen." Another firefighter follows Kevin with oxygen and other equipment. The other three wait in the foyer.

Anna is rooted to the stool, shrinking further into her numb self. She has had Peter put on a movie for the boys.

Kevin's presence fills the house as he walks with Peter.

"Hi, Anna, what's going on? I'm Kevin. Can you tell me what's happening?" He touches her shoulder and squats in front of her. His demeanor reminds her of a kind parent. Peter squats, too, on the other side of her, and puts his hand on her knee.

Tears stream down her face. She pushes out the words. "Why are you guys here? Where's the ambulance?"

"We're the first responders," Kevin says. "Do you need me to call you an ambulance? That's what we'll figure out."

"I can't move my hands or feel my face or lips. I can barely open my mouth. My chest is so tight."

"She thinks she's having a heart attack," Peter says.

"Okay, let's take things one step at a time," Kevin says. "Has this ever happened before?"

"No," says Peter. Anna shakes her head.

"Breathe for me," says Kevin. "Just breathe through your belly, count ten for inhale and ten for exhale. Take your time; slow deep breaths."

The first time Kevin slept with Brenda she wasn't answering her phone. On the last Saturday in September, the Sullivan boys were at the Gallaghers', and, at Alyssa's insistence, Kevin had taken a day off from the Pile. Alyssa told him to drive over and check on her. "Call me when you get there," she had said.

He had found the front door unlocked and Brenda in bed buried under layers of bedding. He'd had to peel them away to get to her. She wouldn't look at him until he embraced and rocked her and said, "Come on, Bren, those boys need you. We're here, I'm here, Alyssa's here, we're all here. I don't know how to do this, either. I should have been there. I'd give anything to have him back. All of them. Or be gone, too."

She had felt so shattered to him that he kept holding her and talking to her, thinking that would be enough, but it hadn't been, and it hadn't stopped there. Only after Brenda started kissing him and pulled him on top of her and it was over did she break her silence with sobs and he cried, too, their apologies mingling moments after their bodies had. When he called Alyssa, he told her that Brenda had gone for a walk and left the house without her phone and that he'd finally found her after forty-five minutes, sitting on a swing in a nearby playground. He told Alyssa, "I'm bringing her back, and we'll have them all for dinner, then I'll run them home. She's a mess. I don't know what else to do." And he'd truly had no idea, especially now, after what he and Brenda had done.

"Of course. Is she all right?" Alyssa said. "I'll tell the boys. She shouldn't be alone. Should they stay here tonight, too? Kevin, tell her of course, and they can all spend the night here if they need to."

That's how it went until they left New York. Alyssa and Brenda were friends, and Kevin felt like there was so little he could do, but what he could do he did, and that meant bedding Brenda and mowing the lawn and hanging the Christmas lights and replacing broken windows when there were stray baseballs. Alyssa did what she could for Brenda, too — took the boys, made food, spent time. He felt both crushing guilt and exempt from it, too. It was beyond insanity — he knew: he would rather cut off his own arm than hurt Alyssa, but he had so much goddamn love to give the living who were left. He loved his dead friend, his dead friend's wife, and their two sons. He loved his own wife and their daughter. He gave Alyssa more attention after he started with Brenda, and he separated what he doled out to her from the rest of his life and absolved himself for it. He was doing what he could, and although Alyssa would never understand — he knew she wouldn't and, God help him, she could never find out — his sleeping with Brenda in no way diminished his love for his wife. They were two different things entirely.

When she ended it in March, after six months, Brenda said she was so grateful to Kevin for bringing her back from the dead. "Go back to your life; it needs you more than I do," she told him. "To keep it up would do more harm than good, and I couldn't live with that. You couldn't, either." She said Kevin helped restore her to the person she really was, and she would join the effort with other widows to stand up and be heard. She would start writing to the legislators and going to meetings at city hall and would do everything she could until there was no more to be done.

Alyssa never found out. He had been careful enough, and Brenda had kept her mouth shut. Kevin didn't think he'd done anything but fuck matters up, but he took Brenda at her word, talked to Jimmy in his mind and in his sleep, begged his forgiveness, and took Alyssa to bed more than he ever had, guilty and grateful that he hadn't left his own wife one way or another.

The Gallaghers stayed in New York until the summer of 2002. Kevin didn't know how he could stand to be in New York on the anniversary, he'd told Alyssa on Saint Patrick's Day. So we'll be gone by then, she'd said, and they were.

"Okay, Anna," Kevin says, "let's check your blood pressure and get some oxygen going. That will help you feel better. Do you have kids?"

She nods.

"Tell me about your kids." He attaches the leads to her legs and arms.

Peter smooths her hair. "Jude is eight, and Brian is ten," she manages. "They're great. They still need their mother. I can't die. Do you have kids? Do you know what's happening to me?"

"Do you know what's happening to her?" Peter says.

"Will you go check on the boys?" Anna says. "I don't want them to freak out."

"They're fine," says Peter. "I'll go in a minute; I don't want to leave you."

"She's okay, if you want to go ahead," Kevin says to Peter.

"Okay, but I'll be right back." Peter kisses Anna's forehead.

"Do you have kids?" she says again.

"My wife and I have three girls," Kevin says. "The women rule the roost at my house. Anna, I think you're having a panic attack. That's what I think, but we'll find out. Keep breathing and try to relax. Everything's okay. Are you under a lot of stress right now? One sixty over one oh four. Your blood pressure is high. That can happen with a panic attack."

Anna's tears keep coming. "That's high for me. I'm usually at one oh two or lower. My father died. He died a month ago. Both my parents are dead now."

"I'm so sorry to hear that," Kevin says. "Were you close? Keep breathing through your nose into your belly. Ten in, ten out."

"No." Anna cries, tucked and immobile. "We weren't. He was a career alcoholic, his father was a drunk, and his father was, too. He lived in New Jersey. My mom died three years ago. I was close to her. That was the worst thing that's ever happened to me. My mother dying. The movers are coming today with their stuff that we shipped. What's the worst thing that's ever happened to you?"

Kevin looks at her pulse ox. "Ninety-seven: that's good, Anna. Is the oxygen helping?"

"Yes," she says. She is so grateful for this kind man. "Thank you. You're so nice." Her tears continue. "What's the worst thing that ever happened to you? Have you lost a parent?"

"Not yet," says Kevin. Even now, not far from the peak of his thoughts are the parades of flags covering empty caskets, the futility amid the dust and debris. "Life throws us all terrible things we have to survive. It seems like you've had more than your share. It would be hard for anyone. Go easy on yourself."

Anna's tears refresh. She wishes she could manage to laugh. *Go easy on yourself.* Her ability to do so has eluded her her whole life. She doesn't even know where she would start. It feels to her like she and this firefighter have been here talking since the beginning of time. It's only the two of them. Peter must still be with the boys, and the other firefighter lingers on the other side of the kitchen.

"What's the worst thing you've ever done?" she says. Her hands are still in rigor, her mouth contracted.

Her question drags him to Jimmy and Brenda. To Brenda's Celtic wedding tattoo—the tree of life—which only Jimmy, Kevin, and her ob-gyn have ever seen.

"I'm a born-and-bred New Yorker," he says. "My list of worst is too long to choose just one. Keep breathing for me. Nice and easy."

Anna's shrunken mouth purses her words. "Oh, Peter and I lived in New York, too. Years ago. That's where we met. We lived in Brooklyn. Nine eleven, my God. Were you there?"

"No," Kevin says. "I wasn't."

"Oh, thank God. I was obsessed. So much devastation," Anna says. "I don't know what I think I have to cry about." She crumples anew. "God, I'm such a baby. I'm sorry."

"Come on, Anna," says Kevin. "You're dealing with so much right now. Look at me. Those boys need you; they need their mom. Just concentrate on breathing. I know it's tough, but try to get out of your head. You're okay. Everything's okay."

"Do you want to know what the worst thing I've ever done is?" says Anna.

"Will it help?" Kevin says. "If it will, you can tell me. Nothing is ever as bad as you think."

"No, it won't, but if I'm dying, I have to get it off my chest," says Anna. Again she wishes she could laugh, now at her own joke. "I wasn't sorry and I wasn't sad when my father died. I was devastated when my mother died, but not when he died."

"Did you have your reasons?" Kevin says. "If you have your reasons, good reason, for something, it's different. Inhale, one to ten."

"I am my father's daughter," Anna says. "I don't think he was sorry when his father died, either. And I drank too much last night. I don't want to turn into my father."

"I'm sure you're nothing like your father," Kevin says. "Your blood pressure is coming down; that's good. Do you want me to get Peter and your kids? You're not dying, Anna, not today. But I'll call an ambulance if you want to go to the hospital. Do you want to go? If you do, I'll wait until they come and I'll ride with you."

Anna feels unmoored. She closes her eyes. She is going to die someday. She wants to feel her mother smooth her hair again, one more time, to talk Anna out of herself as only she knew how to do. How funny to crave being a child again, to desperately want someone else in charge, she thinks. She wants someone to take care of her, differently from the way Peter does, as only a parent can. How cruel to have gone the people who wanted you in this world in the first place. She feels like she needs to get out, to safety, but there is no out, no ride to get off. Life is too hard sometimes, but life is all there is. There is no stop to get off, no place to walk away from and just leave. So many decisions for her to make now. As she sits there, it seems as likely she will make the wrong one as the right one. Her parents' only remaining things are coming soon, and her house is the last place those things will dwell until she and Peter die. And she has no idea where they will go.

"I don't know," she says. Her fears are infinite. This is her decision, in this second, right or wrong, independent of anyone else. There are going to be so many more worries — about the boys getting older, getting in the wrong car on the wrong night; Peter; their marriage; the house; money; the loom of disease — crises she can't even imagine dreading yet. She's not really alone, of course, but she feels like there is no one to help her when she's utterly stuck, someone who has navigated the world before she joined it, who knows exactly what to do. All she wants is her mother, and her absence makes Anna want to scream. She just wants someone to take care of her. She wants a rest from taking care of everyone else.

"Please," says Anna. "Can you just stay for a little while longer? And just sit with me?"

"As long as you want me to," Kevin says. "I'll stay right here."

Her hands are unclenching and her mouth is relaxing — not a lot, but the breathing is working.

She takes another breath and counts. "Do you have a dog?" she says.

"I do," says Kevin. "Emmett. My girls spoil the old guy rotten."

"Oh," Anna says. "That's so nice." She wipes her face. "Will you tell me about Emmett?"

Acknowledgments

I have many people to thank, and language has limits for conveying the depth of my gratitude. This collection would not be possible without you.

Wendy Sherman, my agent and friend, who is the smartest, funniest, loveliest gladiator I ever could have hoped for. Thank you for taking, and continuing to take, such exquisite care of my work and me.

After my first conversation and meeting with Judy Clain, I couldn't imagine a stronger connection or collaboration with an editor. I am so grateful for your faith in this book, and to you and everyone at Little, Brown for making these stories the very best they could be.

Thank you to Win McCormack, Rob Spillman, Lance Cleland, and everyone at Tin House for founding and directing the best writer's conference there is, and thanks most especially to my friend Holly MacArthur, who told me about the workshop where I would ultimately get my education as a writer. This book would not exist without the abundant generosity and razor-sharp skills of Steve Almond, Elissa Schappell, Meg Storey, and Joy Williams, who all gave my writing such careful attention and fine polish during our work together: thank you.

I'm grateful for the unflagging support of writers and colleagues, from both the Tin House and Portland communities, especially Matthew Dickman, Alan Heathcock, Kelly Luce, Shanna Mahin, Lisa Mecham, Jason Maurer, Ian Miller, Olga Zilberbourg, and my Fresno gang.

I am indebted to Bob Olmstead, my first writing teacher, under whose mentorship I built my foundation as a writer and whose encouragement means as much now as it did then.

Thank you to my earliest readers for your dear friendships and for never holding back: Mead Hunter, Vanessa Kauffman, Brooke Noli, and Marne Maykowskyj Nordean.

My greatest thanks to my tribe — Carolyn and Jess, Mike and Ryan — for your love and belief and laughter. The value of your friendships, individually and together, is beyond measure, and you are the very best version of family. It was worth the wait to finally find you.

Finn and Brady, my charming boys, my handsome sons, my most devout fans, you have made me prouder and luckier than I ever thought I could be. I love you a ton and a half million, and more than the world.

Patrick, my touchstone, thank you for every minute of every day, for your fierce love, and for dancing around the world with me.

About the Author

Polly Dugan lives in Portland, Oregon, with her husband and two sons and is a reader at *Tin House* magazine. She has attended the Tin House Writer's Workshop for the past four years and is a former Powell's bookseller. She is currently at work on a novel.

OCEAN COUNTY LIBRARY

3 3 5 0 0 9 9 6 8 5 5 1 8 5

JUN   2014

JACKSON TOWNSHIP BRANCH
Ocean County Library
2 Jackson Drive
Jackson, NJ 08527